About the Author

Mark A. Vance is a veteran airline captain for a major U.S. airline with over 27,000 flying hours. He also has C-Suite experience as the President/CEO of a successful capital management firm. His academic credits include an A.S. and B.S. Degree in Air Commerce/Transportation Technology from Florida Institute of Technology, an M.B.A. Degree in Accounting from Indiana Wesleyan University, an M.S. Degree in Strategic Management from Indiana University, a Graduate Certificate in Treasury Management from Duke University and Graduate Certificates in Aviation Management and Advanced Project Management from Stanford University. He has the academic distinction of *Beta Gamma Sigma* membership, a scholarly entity reserved for the top ten percent of global business school graduates from AACSB accredited institutions.

As a child, he lived as a guest of the Blackfeet Nation on the Blackfeet Indian Reservation in Browning, Montana. He and his wife, of Cherokee Choctaw ancestry, reside in North Carolina. They are committed to the study of God's Word, researching and applying Biblical truth, living in God's will for their lives, and sharing their spiritual insights and experiences. They are also dedicated to honoring the Jack B. Ketchum Bomber Crew of World War II, and the author's late Uncle S/Sgt. Raymond E. Davis.

amazon.com/author/markvance

A cocky, wisecracking, commercial airline pilot has a surreptitious, lifelong relationship with the apparition of a dead relative, killed decades earlier in a military plane crash. When the apparition urges the pilot to solve the mystery of that crash, government censorship and stonewalling ensues, eventually surmounted by confidential information provided by entities disguised as the pilot's dead relative and murdered comrades.

Also by Mark A. Vance

Nonfiction

Flight of the Forgotten - A True Story of Heroism and Betrayal

A Living Memorial to the Jack B. Ketchum Bomber Crew

Available Worldwide

ISBN
E-Book   978-1-7328679-0-1
Softcover   978- 1-7328679-1-8

Book Cover Art
SelfPubBookCovers.com/Viergacht

ANGELS OF LIGHT

Beyond the Veil

By

Mark A. Vance

This story is dedicated to the source of all truth and light.

Forward

Inspired by actual events, this story is a progressive spiritual revelation. It repeatedly pierces the spiritual veil surrounding our physical world and provides graphic, supernatural insight into the powerful, omnipresent world beyond. The underlying narrative serves as a point-blank spiritual antidote, delivered through the sharing of authentic supernatural experiences that are predicated on the author's original work, *Flight of the Forgotten.*

This adaptation of that original work comprises a lifetime of ghostly interactions and other-worldly experiences, that at its zenith yields highly classified official information and lays bare a top-secret government file. The accuracy of the original work's spiritually derived information was used to solve a fifty year old aviation mystery.

Whether that privileged information was derived angelically or satanically is the basis for this spiritual adaptation. The hazard awaiting innocent excursions beyond the veil is a matter every individual must acknowledge and correctly assess. My hope is that *Angels of Light* will serve as a benchmark of spiritual discernment in all manners and modes of supernatural interaction, while also fostering a strong desire to learn more about fundamental spiritual truth.

Characters

- Steve Lacey (Age 3) - Toddler - Nephew of Ray Wilkins, deceased member of the James Tyree World War II Bomber Crew (Black Hameldon Bomber)
- Steve Lacey (Age 8) - Child - Nephew of Ray Wilkins, deceased member of the James Tyree World War II Bomber Crew (Black Hameldon Bomber)
- Steve Lacey (Age 15) - Fledgling Aviator - Nephew of Ray Wilkins, deceased member of the James Tyree World War II Bomber Crew (Black Hameldon Bomber)
- Steve Lacey (Age 20) - Fledgling Aviator - Nephew of Ray Wilkins, deceased member of the James Tyree World War II Bomber Crew (Black Hameldon Bomber)
- Steve Lacey (Age 42) - Airline Captain - Nephew of Ray Wilkins, deceased member of the James Tyree World War II Bomber Crew (Black Hameldon Bomber)
- Ray Wilkins (*Apparition*) - Uncle of Steve Lacey and Ball-Turret Gunner of the James Tyree World War II Bomber Crew (Black Hameldon Bomber)
- James Tyree (*Apparition*) - B-24 Command Pilot - World War II Bomber Crew (Black Hameldon Bomber)
- Robbie Akin - Flight Instructor - Cessna Aircraft
- Michael Carpenter - Resident Psychic - Illinois Society of Spiritualists and Naturalists (Camp Ellis)
- Joyce Lacey - Mother of Steve Lacey
- Elizabeth Wilkins - Mother of Ray Wilkins and Great-Grandmother of Steve Lacey
- William Wilkins - Father of Ray Wilkins and Great-Grandfather of Steve Lacey
- Kay Lacey - Wife of Steve Lacey
- Gladys Spencer - Sister of Ray Wilkins and Grandmother of Steve Lacey
- Eldon Wilson (*Apparition*) - Flight Engineer of the James Tyree World War II (Black Hameldon Bomber Crew)
- Ed Reddick (*Apparition*) - Waist-Gunner of the James Tyree World War II (Black Hameldon Bomber Crew)
- Cole Johnson (*Apparition*) - Co-Pilot of the James Tyree World War II (Black Hameldon Bomber Crew)
- Stephen Coronado (*Apparition*) - Navigator of the James Tyree World War II (Black Hameldon Bomber Crew)
- Brandon Powers (*Apparition*) - Nose-Gunner of the James Tyree World War II (Black Hameldon Bomber Crew)
- Jacob Stewart (*Apparition*) - Radio-Operator of the James Tyree World War II (Black Hameldon Bomber Crew)

- Dennis Weathers (*Apparition*) - Waist-Gunner of the James Tyree World War II (Black Hameldon Bomber)
- Eric Irving (*Apparition*) - Tail-Gunner of the James Tyree World War II (Black Hameldon Bomber Crew)
- Ian McShane - Local Resident/Hiker - Black Hameldon, Moors area, Lancashire, England
- Satan/Lucifer - Feral Head of Demonic Forces, Prince of Darkness, Fallen Angel
- Wohali Rogers - Pastor/Tribal Council Member - Cherokee Nation, Tahlequah, Oklahoma, Husband of Awinita Rogers & Uncle of Kay Lacey
- Awinita Rogers - Cherokee Nation, Tahlequah, Oklahoma, Wife of Wohali Rogers &Aunt of Kay Lacey
- Senator Ashton Bancroft - Senior U.S. Senator - State of Georgia; Senate Select Committee on Intelligence
- Dr. Lenny Williams - Senior Pastor - Local Church, Atlanta, Georgia
- A. J. Williams - B-17 Command Pilot- World War II Bomber Crew
- Dr. David Monroe - Senior Theologian - University Seminary, Atlanta, Georgia
- Edward Hickey - U.S. Government - Office of Strategic Services - European Theater of Operations
- Tom Sturnman - U.S. Government - Office of Strategic Services - European Theater of Operations
- Phil Osterhouse - U.S. Government -Office of Strategic Services - European Theater of Operations
- Nate Watson - U.S. Government -Office of Strategic Services - European Theater of Operations
- Curtis Lemond - U.S. Government - Office of Strategic Services - European Theater of Operations

Table of Contents

PART I

GUARDIAN ANGEL

Chapter One

Masquerade
"And no wonder, for Satan himself masquerades as an Angel of Light."
2nd Corinthians 11:14

It's the Summer of 1969, and three year old Steve Lacey is decades away from attaining anything resembling spiritual discernment. At present, he is immersed in pushing a toy, wooden airplane across the floor of his grandparent's living room in Shelby, North Carolina. Young Lacey stares in fascination at the U. S. Air Force markings and watches the pilot's head spin around and around, as he forces the wheels to turn faster and faster. Nearby, several adults are talking about a deceased relative named Ray, and the mysterious airplane crash that took his life years ago. Their discourse is disjointed and at times rambling, but it eventually turns to Ray's Service Bible, and how a man living in England near the crash site, found Ray's Bible and returned it to the Wilkins family. None of the adults are able to offer a reasonable conjecture that might explain how such a small, fragile item survived unscathed in the flaming wreckage of Ray's World War II bomber.

Young Lacey is unburdened by such weighty concerns as he recklessly pushes the toy airplane at breakneck speed across the soft carpet. In the room with him, but not heard by the adults, a disembodied, beguiling voice begins to cautiously engage him. The spectral voice is male, calm, deliberate, and intensely alluring. It counsels him about the need for caution around all airplanes, asserting that, "anomalies in an airplane sometimes foster sad consequences." The ghostly, disembodied voice behind the peculiar declaration identifies itself as Ray, and continues nurturing the child's attention for the next several minutes. Ultimately, it summarizes its other-worldly mission by boldly proclaiming to three year old Steve Lacey that it will be with him all of his life, especially whenever he is flying a real airplane. The youngster is unmoved by the other-worldly proclamation and continues interacting exclusively with the toy, although slightly less aggressively in response to the ethereal warning. It will be decades before Steve Lacey hears the idiom, "anomalies in an airplane" again. When it recurs, the source of the message will be a three dimensional apparition identifying itself as James Tyree, command pilot of the Black Hameldon Bomber, Uncle Ray's airplane.

Five years later, eight year old Steve Lacey is visiting his great-grandparent's (Ray Wilkins parent's) farm in Shelby, North Carolina for the very first time. Raised in the city, he has no farm experience, and has never been exposed to such a rural environment. It is a real working farm in Western North Carolina, and as a male, he is expected to participate in all the daily chores. With no consideration for his age or city upbringing, his great-grandfather, Grandpa Wilkins rebukes him sharply for failing to properly milk a semi-confused and rather stubborn dairy cow. Wilkins is a man engrossed in the workings of his family farm, with little patience for children or city folk. He is also a man that suffered unimaginable heartache as a result of losing his oldest son, Ray in the war, but none of that was apparent or mattered to his great-grandson this hot Summer afternoon. In the eyes of Grandpa Wilkins, Steve is just a bungling child, incapable of performing even the simplest farm task without continuous and sometimes harsh correction.

Dejected, Steve is committed to leaving the Wilkins farm immediately, as he retreats to the farmhouse, seeking reassurance from his mother. The living room of the small, wood frame farmhouse is filled with adult relatives, but he remains determined as he states openly and unequivocally that he wants to leave. In response, his great-grandmother, Grandma Wilkins (Ray's mother) intervenes, takes him by the hand and begins showing him around her home. Her efforts to distract him are not immediately successful, but his attention is soon drawn to a picture on the wall of several men in front of a World War II bomber. Grandma Wilkins notices his instant fascination with the picture and states proudly, "that's Ray and his crew!" as he continues staring wide eyed at the black and white picture. It reminds him of his favorite television show, *12 o' clock High,* and he struggles to separate fantasy from the family reality about to unfold in front of him.

His mother, Joyce Lacey joins the conversation, assuring Grandma Wilkins that her son's interest in the picture is predicated on the *12 o'clock High* television show. She then begins to clarify to him, exactly who his great-grandmother is referring to.

"Ray was your uncle, your grandmother's brother." she stated succinctly, as he nodded and without hesitation pointed to his Uncle Ray among the nine men in the picture. He then asks innocently, "where is Ray now? I can hear him, but I almost never see him."

"What?" his mother exclaimed with a start, taking him by the hand and leading him away from the picture.

"Where is he now?" he repeated, as his mother tried desperately to distract him and ignore the question.

"He's gone, honey." Grandma Wilkins replied sadly, the twinkle in her eye fading as she spoke.

"Gone?" he countered, sensing something was radically wrong. "But he can't be gone! He talks to me all the time!"

"Oh, my!" Grandma Wilkins exclaimed as she recoiled at the pronouncement and stared at him in awe for several moments. Slowly, the twinkle in her misty blue eyes began to return.

"He's really interested in airplanes! It's just like his favorite television show *12 o'clock High* to him!" Joyce Lacey stammered, trying desperately to put Uncle Ray's mother at ease.

Smiling knowingly, Grandma Wilkins then leaned forward and patted him on the head, gazing curiously into his eyes.

"He talks to you?" she prompted, as he nodded innocently. "Is … is he all right?" she asked cautiously.

"Yes!" he exclaimed. "He says I'm going to be a jet pilot when I grow up!"

Both of the women are dumbfounded and unnerved by the eerie revelation as they stare at one another in shock, but neither utters a sound. Moments later, Grandma Wilkins is inspired to take him by the hand and lead him to a small bookshelf in the corner of her dining room. His mother follows hesitantly, a few steps behind. Upon reaching the bookshelf, Grandma Wilkins retrieves a small, well-worn Bible and holds it to her heart before declaring,"this is Ray's Bible. It was with him on all his missions and also when he died. A man in England sent it to our family. He discovered it near Ray's airplane. Someday, Ray's Bible will be yours. Ray would want you to have it."

He reaches out and carefully touches the small, mysterious sounding book. The immediate sensation of something supernatural is undeniable, even at such a tender age. He feels positive energy emanating from its binding and notices that the look of apprehension has completely disappeared from his mother's face. Moments later, Grandpa Wilkins enters the small wood frame farmhouse, offering his great-grandson a pronounced and unmistakable scowl. Still leery of his great-grandfather, Steve then asks innocently,"is this book's power strong enough to work on Grandpa Wilkins?"

"Oh, probably, but he's pretty set in his ways." Grandma Wilkins replied, still displaying the pronounced twinkle in her eyes and offering him a comforting smile that he will always remember.

In the early Summer of 1981, New Orleans Lakefront Airport is alive with activity. For fifteen year old Steve Lacey, this is destined to be a historic day. The training syllabus for his flying lesson today stated rather matter of fact, "first unassisted solo", a decidedly anticlimactic billing for such a monumental event. His flight instructor, Robbie Akin, is obviously taking great pains to mirror the nonchalant billing on the training syllabus, as he jokingly asks him, "do you think you can get the airplane around the pattern without killing yourself?" Before Steve can respond, Akin feels his pulse and declares, "don't worry, young man, apprehension is normal!" prior to imparting a plethora of last minute instructions and much needed encouragement.

After Steve lands the small Cessna unassisted for the third time in a row, Akin orders him to taxi the tiny aircraft to the side of the runway.

"Okay, that's good! I'll get out here!" he declares.

Moments later, Robbie Akin exits the Cessna, turns and grasps Steve's hand with a firm, good luck handshake, before departing from view. After watching his instructor depart, Steve carefully latches the door closed, and then slowly scans the tiny cockpit. He has never felt more alone at any time in his life as he begins taxiing the nimble little trainer for his first unassisted takeoff.

Suddenly, the seat next to him is filled with a very familiar, ethereal figure, Uncle Ray, who eagerly greets him, implores him to relax, and then without hesitation begins coaching and directing him like a stand in flight instructor. Uncle Ray also begins unleashing a tidal wave of encouragement, including the well rehearsed mantra that Steve longs to someday become a jet pilot. What began moments before as his first unassisted solo flight, filled with apprehension and semi-dread, quickly morphs into a beautiful, shared experience with a trusted angelic friend, relative, and fellow airman.

"We've been waiting for this moment for years! You know you can do it! You'll be just fine! All you have to do is concentrate and do exactly what I tell you!" Uncle Ray declared, as Steve listened in speechless reverence.

"There's a first time for everything. No need to worry. It's just another step on your path to success. You want to be a jet pilot someday, don't you?"Uncle Ray continued prompting.

"I do want to be a jet pilot." Steve echoed.

"Well then?" Uncle Ray urged, as Steve began recovering from the initial shock of his uncle's ghostly presence and started performing the mandatory engine run up.

"I'm just here to help. Relax … everything is going to be fine." Uncle Ray offered reassuringly, as Steve nodded in silence and struggled to successfully complete the before takeoff checklist.

Minutes later, taxiing onto the runway for takeoff, the sensation of having Uncle Ray beside him on his supposedly first unassisted solo flight is transformed into the memory of a lifetime. The first unassisted solo flight is an enormous milestone in any aviator's life, not something shared or experienced by another person. Sharing this experience with Uncle Ray completely alleviates all of his trepidation as he carefully pulls back on the control wheel and the little Cessna trainer staggers into the air.

"Okay, now I have to get this thing back on the ground. My life depends on it." he declares, as the little trainer climbs slowly to pattern altitude.

"I'm right here. Nothing bad is going to happen. Just concentrate, and do exactly what I tell you." Uncle Ray prompts, as they begin circling the traffic pattern for his first solo landing.

"Carry a little extra power on this one. Keep the nose up. Easy … easy." Uncle Ray encouraged, as the little trainer touched down smoothly and Steve manually lowered the elevator pitch trim and applied full power for the touch and go.

"Not bad." Uncle Ray encouraged, as the little Cessna climbed back up to pattern altitude.

Minutes later, following his second successful solo landing, Steve is feeling completely at ease, and actually enjoying himself as he and Uncle Ray fly around the traffic pattern together. Uncle Ray emphasizes repeatedly that he will always be there whenever Steve needs him and that he will never have anything to fear in an airplane.

After five successful solo takeoffs and landings, Steve slows the aircraft to a full stop and taxis carefully toward Robbie Akin, his awaiting flight instructor. At this point, Steve is thoroughly enjoying the experience and hesitant to see it all end. The reality of what has just transpired has not yet settled in his consciousness.

"This is where I leave you." Uncle Ray stated very matter of fact. "Remember … you're going to be a jet pilot someday." he reminds him one more time, before vanishing into thin air.

As Steve approaches his awaiting flight instructor, Robbie Akin is grinning from ear to ear. His instructor opens the aircraft door and exclaims, "congratulations!" shaking his hand again and climbing back into the right seat of the tiny cockpit. Steve's mood is more reflective than jubilant, as he taxis the aircraft to the parking area, shuts down the engine, and slowly begins to contemplate what just occurred. He is well aware that it hadn't really been an unassisted first solo flight at all. Uncle Ray had been next to him the entire time, coaching, encouraging, and directing him. With the apparition of his deceased uncle in the right seat next to him, he had just successfully flown around the traffic pattern five times. For a brief moment, he wonders whether Uncle Ray's perpetual coming and going might be part of some larger cosmic plan. Everyone has deceased ancestors, but he never heard of anybody taking them on a training flight in an airplane decades after they died.

"Can I give you a lift?" Robbie Akin asks as they finish tying down the Cessna trainer and completing the essential paperwork.

"I don't think my bike will fit in the back of your car." he replied, gesturing toward his two wheel transportation resting against the side of the hangar.

"Your bike?" the instructor echoes. "Oh, that's right! You don't start driver's education until next Summer!" he joked, as the two of them begin walking toward the operations trailer.

Every few steps, Steve glances over his shoulder at the little Cessna, and begins to wonder if the life he'd chosen might indeed be part of something much bigger, something involving Uncle Ray. After all, Ray had reiterated several times that he would always be there whenever he was flying. This was just the latest unearthly encounter with Uncle Ray, one of many throughout his young lifetime.

Bicycling home, his thoughts drift back to Shelby, North Carolina, his Grandma Wilkins, and the twinkle in her blue eyes that Summer afternoon as she talked about her son, Ray. Today had been a supernatural day too, just like the feeling he had when he first touched Ray's Bible. Long before he reaches home, he is overwhelmingly convinced that Uncle Ray is his guardian angel, possessing divine power, sent directly from Heaven to always keep him safe in an airplane.

Three weeks later, he returns to Shelby, North Carolina for an extended Summer visit with his grandparents. Throughout his stay, he enjoys the time of his life, doing things city kids only dream about, and also getting to know his grandparents better at the same time. His days are filled with semi-laborious tasks, and there are plenty of them on his grandfather's small farm, but the long Summer evenings leave him free to pursue leisure activities that really matter to him, like hunting and fishing. It was simple and pure, as close to Heaven as he could imagine at such a young age. Occasionally, he would sit on a fence post at his grandparent's farm and stare longingly at the contrails lining the sky above him. He knew that someday that fast paced, high flying world would be his too, and that he would be making those contrails instead of just daydreaming about them.

Later that evening, at his grandparent's dining table, he is still thinking about that exotic world of high flying contrails, when the conversation suddenly turns to airplanes and how he became so intensely interested in them.

"Were you daydreaming about airplanes and flying again?" his grandmother asked outright.

"Yes, I guess so." he replied sheepishly, finding words difficult all of a sudden.

"Where did all this airplane business come from? You didn't hear about them from any of us." she charged.

"Oh, it's always been about either baseball or airplanes with me, Grandma. Don't you remember?"

"Well, I certainly remember all the model airplanes you built when you were younger, and how you used to live for *12 o'clock High*, but you aren't still thinking about becoming a pilot when you grow up, are you?" she asked point-blank, staring at him with obvious concern.

"Well, actually I've already started learning to fly." he replied.

"Learning to fly?" she gasped.

"Yes, I soloed three weeks ago. I'm flying Cessna's now, but someday I'm going to be a jet pilot!" he announced emphatically.

"A jet pilot? But … aren't jet pilots trained in the service?" his grandmother asked apprehensively.

"If that's what it takes, then that's what I'll do." he declared without hesitation, watching his grandmother suddenly look away in distress. "What is it?" he asked, trying to interpret her reaction to his proclamation about flying jets.

"Come with me. There's something I want to show you." she ordered, rising from the dinner table and leading him out of the dining room and down a small hallway. Halfway down, she pointed to a large, framed photograph on the wall and asked pointedly, "do you know who that is?" as he stared at the black and white photograph and nodded silently.

"And do you know what happened to my brother?" she asked sadly, fighting tears back as she brushed a hint of dust from the photograph.

"I know there was a crash, but I don't know what actually happened to him." he replied, cautiously.

"We never found out what really happened. His bomber exploded on the way home from England and everyone was killed." she said mournfully, wiping tears from her eyes. "And now you want to be a pilot?"

"Well …" he stammered, at a loss for words.

"Today is the thirty-sixth anniversary of his crash and it still feels like yesterday." she continued, staring at the photograph as he began feeling more awkward than ever.

"It doesn't have to be like that, Grandma. It's … it's … something I feel driven to do." he stammered, as his grandmother eyed him suspiciously.

Eventually, after a heartfelt exchange lasting several minutes, his grandmother surprises him by withdrawing her flagrant objection and even offering her resigned support for his stated goal, under two conditions.

"Well, I suppose I can stand it if you say you have to do it and that it's your true calling in life. But promise me that you'll always be extremely careful and that you won't fly in outer space. I don't think I could handle that." she said, squeezing his hand for emphasis.

"You've got a deal, Grandma. No outer space and I'll be extra careful just for you." he promised, hugging her tightly to reassure her. "Did anyone ever try to find out what happened to Uncle Ray and his crew?" he asked curiously, nodding at the photograph.

"None of the families were told anything, except the date it happened, and that there was a fire and explosion." she replied, readjusting the photograph's slight cant in its place of honor on her wall.

"Ray is okay, Grandma. He's around me all the time and talks to me regularly." he said softly, as his grandmother stared at him with a mixture of apprehension and disbelief.

"He's the main reason I feel driven to become a pilot. I don't know why exactly. I just know that it has something to do with Uncle Ray."

His grandmother paused momentarily, and then reached into a nearby nightstand and withdrew a small, well-worn Bible from the wooden drawer. He recognizes it immediately.

"This was Ray's Bible when he was in service." she declared. "I inherited it when your Grandma Wilkins died. The local church sent them to all the boys in service from this area during the war. It was returned to our family by an Englishman living near the crash site. His letter said that it was open to *John 3:16* when he discovered it. It's truly a miracle that it survived the war and the crash. No one can explain how that happened. The War Department telegram said there was a fire and explosion aboard the airplane before it crashed."

He reaches out and touches the small, miracle book, just as he had many years before when Grandma Wilkins first shared it with him. Positive energy quickly begins coursing through his senses, just as it did the first time he touched it. His thoughts return for a moment to that day years prior, with Grandma Wilkins, and how this small book brought the twinkle back to her misty blue eyes.

"Your Grandma Wilkins wanted you to have Ray's Bible." she said emphatically. "She asked me to hold on to it until you were old enough to understand its significance. It's truly a supernatural book, beyond just surviving the war and the explosion and fire. It helps people understand things, important things like truth, right and wrong, living in the light, and the meaning of life."

He is humbled by the heartfelt gesture and reverently accepts Ray's Bible from his grandmother.

"Promise me that you'll read it regularly." she pleaded. "It will help you understand this world and God's will for your life."

Steve nods and replies thoughtfully, "I'm sure Uncle Ray would like that too. He's kind of like my guardian angel, Grandma. I'll read his Bible for both of you.

\

Chapter Two

Sins of the Fathers

"Behold, I show you a mystery."   *1ˢᵗ Corinthians 15:51*

Five years later, twenty year old Steve Lacey is a commercial seaplane pilot in Southeastern Louisiana, flying sunrise to sunset, building flight hours toward his goal of becoming a jet pilot. That goal has become the driving force in his life, and he has taught himself to regard the hazardous nature of seaplane flying as just another obstacle to overcome and master. He is overly confidant in his present circumstance, due to the reassuring words of Ray Wilkins, that, "he will never have anything to fear in an airplane." Steve is resting heavily on those words again today as he watches the ground crew strap oil drilling pipe with explosive heads to the floats of his airplane.

Donning a Mae West, he starts the Cessna's engine and carefully glides the seaplane down the wooden ramp into the awaiting canal. Moments later, he is airborne, in an overloaded Cessna, heavily laden with explosive drilling pipe. Leveling at 500 feet, he flies westward uneventfully for the next forty minutes. Approaching the Atchafalaya Swamp however, the weather begins to deteriorate and he is forced to fly lower and lower to remain below the clouds. Over the next several minutes, the seaplane is continually forced to fly progressively lower, eventually down to a mere 200 feet above the terrain. In addition, Steve is engrossed in deviating around heavy rain showers and lightning that surround the small Cessna in all quadrants.

The overweight Cessna soon becomes engulfed in heavy rain showers and lighting, rocking wildly from side to side. Steve is apprehensive that the air to air lightning and explosive laden drilling pipe he is carrying could become a volatile mixture, and he feels static electricity rising inside the airplane. Caught in the precarious position of flying low over unforgiving terrain, where oil drilling platforms stretch hundreds of feet into the air, and with static electricity rising inside the cockpit, he finds himself utterly dependent on Ray Wilkins assurance that, "he will never have anything to fear in an airplane."

For the next several minutes, heavy rain pounds mercilessly on the windshield and lightning dances around the heavily laden aircraft. The Cessna is bracketing a westerly heading as the weather steadily deteriorates with each passing mile. Forced to fly still lower, down to a mere 100 feet above the terrain, Steve slows the airspeed to provide reaction time if an oil drilling platform suddenly materializes ahead. For the next several minutes, the clouds and heavy rain showers continue to worsen, forcing the Cessna lower and lower, until Steve is flying only 30 feet above the Atchafalaya Swamp, an altitude where everything is a potential hazard.

Only seconds after leveling the Cessna at 30 feet above the massive swamp, the right wing is hit by a tremendous lightning bolt that traverses the entire wing and slashes across the Cessna's forward instrument panel. Temporarily blinded by the enormous flash, Steve feels the airplane shudder from the violent onslaught. Losing visual perception, he finds himself suddenly battling spatial disorientation, in addition to the surrounding severe weather. To compound the developing crisis, the acrid smell of burning electrical wire fills the air, and he struggles to find sufficient air to breathe. Desperate to call out to God for help, his lungs are filled with toxic smoke and devoid of breath. In his mind, he is screaming as loud as he can, but inside the seaplane, the only audible sound is engine and wind noise.

Suddenly, he feels another pair of hands on the controls and hears a strangely familiar voice. Uncle Ray immediately begins offering much needed reassurance that everything will be all right, but suggests that he needs to start an immediate left turn to avoid more severe weather. Uncle Ray's hands guide Steve's hands through the left turn as the purposely slowed Cessna responds sluggishly. Steve's vision remains badly blurred and narrowed by the lightning flash and toxic smoke filling the airplane. He is however able to discern sergeant stripes on the sleeve grasping the control wheel around him. Uncle Ray continues assuring him that they will be out of the severe weather soon as his ghostly hands guide him on the controls. Throughout the other-worldly encounter, Steve is subordinate, but intensely emotional, as he exclaims,

"Ray! Is .. is it really you? How did you know? What's happening to me, Ray? I can't see! I can't breathe!"

"Hold on! You're going to be fine! Crack a window!" Uncle Ray directs, as Steve's eyes focus on the U.S. Eighth Air Force patch on Uncle Ray's left shoulder. Instinctively, Steve fumbles for the tiny handle that positions the side window. As he feels it fill his hand, he forces the tiny window open into the slipstream. Fresh air and deafening engine noise immediately fill the cockpit as his lungs respond to the sudden influx of much needed air. Uncle Ray remains all business, unflappable, and totally unemotional as he helps him gently ease the Cessna back up to 500 feet, where together their hands hold the seaplane level for the next several minutes.

When the Cessna finally exits the hazardous weather, Steve's vision begins to clear and his eyes begin darting around the cockpit, searching intently for Uncle Ray. To his dismay, he finds himself alone once again in the seaplane, as his gaze finally settles on the flight instruments in front of him and he grasps the control wheel tightly to keep his hands from shaking. He is motionless and speechless for the next several minutes, as the near-death experience and ghostly encounter with his late uncle wash over him.

When he is finally able to collect himself, he closes the side-window and resumes flying the original westerly heading. Minutes later, the Cessna is bathed in bright afternoon sunlight and he instinctively checks to make sure that the explosive drilling pipe remains secure. With his hands still shaking from the adrenaline surge, his destination, Lake Charles, Louisiana begins to appear in the afternoon haze, just beyond the horizon.

By the early Spring of 1996, Steve has realized his goal of becoming a jet pilot, and has risen rapidly through the ranks of a major U.S. airline. At age 29, he is one of the youngest commercial jet airline captains in the country. He and his wife, Kay reside in the Atlanta area, and they have grown accustomed to the erratic nature of Steve's flight schedule, and his extended time away from home. The perpetual coming and going makes telephone contact a valuable tool, and he is on the phone as usual this morning, checking in with Kay. He is perplexed by the sound in her voice and astounded when she begins to convey the unearthly reason behind it. Kay Lacey is not inclined to exaggerate, embellish, or even tease regarding such matters, and he knows immediately that something is very, very wrong.

"Calm down and just tell me what happened." he prompts, trying to help his wife regain her composure. "Whatever it is, we'll deal with it."

"There … there was a man here!" she stammered.

"What man? Where?" he demanded.

"Here! In the house!" she exclaimed.

"Is he gone? Did you call the police?" he suggested forcefully.

After an extended pause, his wife collects herself enough to respond.

"It wasn't an ordinary intruder. He was just here for a few seconds and then he vanished into thin air right before my eyes." she said timidly. "He was a ghost, and he was wearing a World War II military flying uniform."

"Where was he?"

"In front of the portable fan in the living room, the one we leave on for the dogs. He was just standing there in the doorway in front of the fan, smiling at me."

"I don't know what to say …" Steve uttered.

"There's more." she continued. "You know that picture in your office of your Uncle Ray and his crew?

"Yes."

"It was one of them." she said emphatically. "Not your uncle, but one of the other men in his crew. I thought I recognized his face, so I went upstairs to your office and I looked at the picture just to make sure. He's standing in the back row."

"Uh-huh." Steve managed.

"I'm certain it was him." she declared. "He was here in our home."

"Did he say anything?"

"No. He just stood in the doorway smiling at me. It was very unnerving." she insisted.

"I'm sure he doesn't mean any harm. If he's one of Uncle Ray's crew, he has to be a friend." Steve insisted.

"It's still unsettling." she replied, obviously unmoved by his attempt at a positive explanation.

A little over a year later, Steve is at the pinnacle of his airline career. Ghostly interactions with Uncle Ray and other members of his crew have subsided and Steve has become thoroughly engrossed in day to day airline flying. His thoughts this evening are on jet operations as he taxis onto the runway for a west departure. Air traffic is heavy at Boston's Logan International Airport, and several flights jam the tower frequency with radio transmissions. His flight is given takeoff clearance and begins rolling down the long, westerly runway. The setting sun directly in front of them, masks the developing danger ahead.

Accelerating through 100 knots, two thousand feet prior to a runway intersection, he hears a frantic radio warning and sees a large turboprop aircraft suddenly materialize to his left. The frantic radio warning is from the turboprop, which is in an all out, but obviously futile effort to stop prior to the runway intersection. His own aircraft is too fast to stop, too slow to fly safely, and a collision with the turboprop at the intersection is suddenly imminent. In response, he pulls aggressively on the Boeing's control column and forces the otherwise ill-fated aircraft into the air, narrowly missing the turboprop as it flashes by beneath him.

The stick-shaker activates immediately, warning him of an impending stall. The sluggish Boeing jet begins wallowing alarmingly from side to side, barely under control. Ahead, the blinding sunset masks the skyscrapers in the downtown Boston area, a mere two miles away. He cannot turn to avoid the buildings and risk stalling the aircraft. They have survived the harrowing near-miss encounter, but are now on the ragged edge of losing total control of the airplane. The intense sunlight prevents him from scanning the flight instruments directly in front of him, and he must steal angled glances at the copilot's flight instruments, while also searching visually in the sun for the skyscrapers in downtown Boston. The blinding sunlight and impending sense of failure causes tears to flow down his cheeks as he struggles desperately to keep the big jet airborne.

In a familiar refrain throughout much of his life, Uncle Ray suddenly appears. The ghostly apparition is only heard and seen by him, as he continues issuing commands and flying the airplane on the ragged edge of control. Uncle Ray's sense of humor is a welcome response to their nearly hopeless situation as he very anticlimactically states …

"You do have a way of making me feel needed. May I suggest a shallow turn to the left, Captain?"

The aircraft responds halfheartedly, as Steve begins executing the slow, left turn, with tears still flowing and the stick-shaker continuing unabated. Uncle

Ray's calm demeanor quickly becomes infectious as he continues directing the shallow left turn, assuring Steve that control will soon return.

"Let's get the gear up!" Uncle Ray directs, followed seconds later by, "okay, you can stop turning now."

As the wings level, the stick-shaker suddenly ceases, the skyscrapers of downtown Boston are no longer a threat, and the aircraft begins to accelerate normally. Uncle Ray surveys the scene briefly and then calmly asserts, "it looks like everything is under control once again. You know, Steve, I will always be here whenever you need me, especially in an airplane." he said emphatically, with a customary wry smile, before cryptically adding, "when the time is right however, I will be back to ask for your help on a very, very, important matter."

Steve is shaken by the experience and utterly speechless as he watches Uncle Ray slowly fade from sight like he had so many times before.

Four months later, Steve is at home in Atlanta, when the first indication that the very important matter Uncle Ray alluded to had actually arrived. The indication comes in the form of an odd query from his wife, Kay, while he is reading the local newspaper. Approaching him late one evening, she asks bluntly, "do you know anyone killed in a fire?"

"Not that I can recall. What's this all about?"

She replies hesitantly that although she knows it is taboo, she went for a reading the previous day with two highly regarded psychics. Both insisted that someone killed in a fire was trying desperately to communicate with her husband.

"What kind of a fire … a house fire?" he prompted, assuming it was some sort of natural calamity.

"They didn't say what kind of fire, only that the person trying to communicate with you did not die of the fire, but was surrounded by fire when they died."

He ponders that revelation for a few moments and then dismisses it with a highly skeptical assessment of the two supposedly gifted psychics.

"I hope you didn't pay too much for that tidbit of generality." he asserted, unaware that Uncle Ray and his crew were killed on impact when their bomber plunged directly into the ground amid a tremendous flash fire. Seizing on the query from Kay, he withdraws Ray's Bible from a nearby drawer, searches for the passage regarding psychics and mediums, and reiterates the Biblical prohibition against such activity. Both of them are unaware at the time that Ray's Bible only survived the impending fiery crash because it was expelled from the doomed bomber as it was self destructing in mid-air. A philosophical discussion between them ensues, regarding Biblical directives, possible exceptions to Biblical directives, and whether psychic messages received in such a manner have an angelic or potentially satanic origin.

Two weeks later, Captain Steve Lacey is approaching the Bradley International Airport, Windsor-Locks, Connecticut, at night in a rainstorm with strong, gusty winds. In 1945, the Bradley International Airport was the recovery point for all the heavy bombers of the U.S. Eighth Air Force returning from England after World War II. Thousands of homesick, young airmen, including the James Tyree Bomber Crew, were routed through Bradley International Airport.

Using airborne weather radar, he successfully deviates around the more intense rain showers, aligns the instrument landing system for the approach, and begins descending. His attention is suddenly diverted by an affable greeting over his right shoulder from a very familiar voice. After offering his traditional greeting, Uncle Ray continues unabated, stating very matter of fact,

"I've been trying to tell you that it's time Steve … time for that seed we planted in you years ago to bear fruit. It's for all the families. My crew needs your help. Our families need to know what happened to us and why we didn't land here in 1945. We will help you uncover the truth, if you will just share it with all our families."

Steve nods silently and repeatedly … his attention divided between Uncle Ray's words and successfully completing the challenging approach and landing. He battles the fluctuating airspeed and gusty crosswinds all the way down the final approach to a smooth landing on the rain soaked runway. As the aircraft slows, he feels the anti-skid system working against the aircraft's tendency to hydroplane. When they finally reach taxi speed, he exits the runway and begins taxiing the jetliner to the airport terminal. Moments later, his copilot gestures toward a large hangar and corresponding static display area near the airport boundary.

"That must be an air museum of some kind." the copilot declared. "That looks like a World War II bomber! You don't see many of those around any more!"

Steve follows the copilot's gesture, and notices several young men standing beside a World War II bomber on static display in front of the large hangar. He points them out to the copilot, but none of them are apparently visible to anyone except him.

"You must have better eyes than I do, Skipper." the copilot suggests as Steve rides the brakes and slows the jet's taxi speed to a crawl. He then stares in fascination as the large group of men offers a unified salute when his aircraft passes. The wind and rain do not appear to have any effect on them and each man is bathed in an eerie glow with no apparent light source. Peering against the jet's side-window, he notices that Uncle Ray is now standing among the large group of men and he recalls the picture on Grandma Wilkins wall many years ago, the same picture now hanging in his office at home. Their faces are eerily familiar, and they are all standing directly in front of him, decades later, at Bradley International Airport, Windsor Locks, Connecticut. None of them appear to have aged a day since the James Tyree Bomber Crew photograph was taken, just prior to the start of their combat tour in 1944.

Chapter Three

Quagmire

"Have nothing to do with the works of darkness, but expose them instead."

Ephesians 5:11

Six weeks later, a local resident of Black Hameldon, Moors area, Lancashire, England, is hiking near the crash site of an American World War II bomber. For decades, the Moors area has been a hotbed of ghostly encounters and supernatural activity. Reports of entire villages of ghost like people materializing and disappearing at will are common, and the number of travelers that have disappeared in the Moors area, never to be seen again, is legendary. Ian McShane is undeterred by all the reports of supernatural activity, focused intently on a challenge issued the previous evening by a Scotsman at the Damion Pub. Black Hameldon residents are quite familiar with a long standing dare to anyone willing to hike alone to the local crash site of an American World War II bomber and return with a detailed photograph to prove their heroism and sense of adventure.

Ian McShane has ignored the challenge for years, until last evening, when a patron from Scotland offered fifty pounds British Sterling to anyone that dared produce such a photograph. The Scotsman avowed that World War II crash sites are common in Scotland, but that the Scottish people are not afraid of them. Filled with liquid courage, he taunted everyone in the Damion Pub regarding the Black Hameldon Bomber, igniting a desire in Ian McShane to prove him wrong about English manhood, and penalize him fifty pounds British Sterling in the process.

After a forty-five minute climb up the steep, narrow hiking trail, McShane is nearing the crest of a ridge overlooking the crash site of the Black Hameldon Bomber. Minutes later, when he finally reaches that crest, he gazes down in awe at the shattered remains of an American World War II bomber, glistening in the bright afternoon sunlight directly below him. He grasps his camera and begins photographing the wreckage from the crest of the ridge overlooking the bomber's debris field. He knows that he must descend the backside of the ridge to get close enough to the actual wreckage to ensure a detailed photograph worthy of fifty pounds British Sterling.

Easing over the crest, he carefully begins the downward trek to the main portion of the bomber's wreckage. Suddenly, his trek is interrupted by ghostly, unseen hands that begin pushing and shoving him aggressively backwards. He finds himself instantly helpless against the unexpected onslaught and pummeled repeatedly by vicious, hostile strikes that he cannot see or defend against. The demonic aggression rapidly escalates to invisible clinched fists as McShane staggers backwards from the repetitive, powerful blows. Swinging his own fists wildly in a desperate attempt to fend off the savage, other-worldly attack, his efforts only serve to enrage the hellish presence and intensify their violent assault.

Beaten incessantly as he tries to retreat, McShane suddenly loses his balance and falls backwards down the steep hiking trail that he had ascended so purposefully only minutes before. Distance offers no reprieve however, as the unearthly assault continues unabated and he falls repeatedly in stages down the steep incline. Screaming in agony as his lower body impacts the ground at a sharp angle and his right leg fractures, he still finds no respite. Wallowing pitifully on the ground, he feels his shoulders unceremoniously contorted to the point of separation as the vicious assault continues to escalate. Desperate to get away at all cost, McShane falls forcefully down another portion of the steep hiking trail. Each pause in his runaway fall quickly precipitates another sudden onset beating and an encore of extreme physical torment. Eventually, after free falling in stages over 300 feet, his vision blackens and the searing pain in his broken right leg causes him to lose consciousness. Laying motionless beside the Black Hameldon Bomber hiking trail, rescue workers finally locate Ian McShane thirty-six hours later and begin rendering much needed life saving aid to his badly mangled body.

It's March 1998, and after months of stonewalling by the U.S. Air Force to his request for an uncensored accident report, Steve is getting desperate. Convinced that his effort to uncover the truth enjoys heavenly support, he blatantly ignores Biblical directives against such activity and visits Camp Ellis, at the Illinois Society of Spiritualists and Naturalists. His trip is a deliberately focused attempt to bypass US Government stonewalling and censorship, and to uncover the hidden truth about the Black Hameldon Bomber crash and the James Tyree Crew.

He has a meeting scheduled this afternoon with Michael Carpenter, a renowned resident psychic at the well regarded facility. Both men are approximately the same age, and their meeting is arranged as a one on one session. An hour later, when the session finally concludes, Carpenter will confide in him that he has never seen so many spiritual entities trying to communicate with one living being in all the years he has been practicing. Carpenter likens the spiritual information overload he experienced during the session to everyone at a football game trying to enter the stadium at the same time, through a single entrance. He opens the dramatic session with an amazing declaration …

"Someone here wants to say hello. Do you know anybody named Ray?"

Steve is too stunned to speak, but manages to nod silently as the psychic continues …

"Ray is saying that it took a long time, but now you're finally in a position where you can help them and that's why they contacted you. Ray is joking about you not thinking that this was all your idea. He also says that it was quite a reunion when your grandmother passed." the psychic relayed, as a speechless Steve Lacey can only nod in amazement.

"There is someone else with us today. There is a James Tyree here. Would you like to ask him anything?"

Steve seizes the tremendous opportunity to ask the deceased bomber pilot exactly what happened to his bomber and his crew that fateful day in 1945. Michael Carpenter relays, "James Tyree wants you and all the families to know that it wasn't his fault. They were headed home after the war in Europe ended. Their combat tour was finished and they were coming home, expecting to be separated from the service. The cause of their crash was two timed-explosive charges and all the man made anomalies they were having with the airplane."

Steve is stunned at the revelation of sabotage and can only stare at the psychic in utter disbelief.

"James Tyree says that he and another crewmen saw plans for a weapon of mass destruction being loaded aboard the C-54 transport plane they were supposed to ride home as passengers. The weapon in question was capable of killing thousands of people at a time, but it did not destroy property. The lie about them being killed while riding home as passengers on a C-54 transport plane was the official cover story created by the U.S. Government, specifically the Office of Strategic Services."

"I'd like the names of everyone responsible." Steve stated flatly.

"James Tyree wants you to know that they are not seeking revenge and that they have had plenty of time to adjust to their new situation. What they want is for all their families to know exactly what happened to them and for people to understand that a sacrifice made out of love of country is a sacred gift ... I'm hearing from someone else now ... Jacob Stewart. He says he was the radio-operator. Jacob is telling me that you will never be able to prove what really happened to their bomber because the government file in question is classified top-secret and it will never be declassified. He says you need to watch for Nora."

Steve asks for clarification regarding the radio-operator's statement, as both he and the psychic initially assume that Nora is the proper name of someone connected with the tragedy.

"Jacob Stewart is explaining that he was referring to NARA; National Archives and Records Administration and the soon to be declassified information concerning the post war period in Europe."

Carpenter then announces, "James Tyree is showing me something about the airplane now. He is wearing a leather jacket, like pilots always wear, and pointing to an open area in the belly of the airplane. He says that it's where one of the timed-explosive charges detonated, causing a tremendous fire. He says that the plot to murder them involved a crash at sea. Because they departed behind schedule and were circling in response to the anomalies they were having with the airplane, the crash occurred well inland."

Carpenter then stuns Lacey by offering, "Ray is now showing me how he used to talk to you when you were a small child playing with your airplane on the floor."

That memory was so personal to Steve that he had never told another living soul about it and he is completely overwhelmed by Carpenter's statement, especially having it referred to by someone he met only two hours before. He stares blankly at Carpenter for several moments, in stunned silence, trying to process all that he just heard.

"There's something James Tyree wants me to ask you to do. He would very much like for you to deliver a special message to his wife, Jennie."

"Anything I can do ..." Steve replies awkwardly, unnerved by the session's dramatic revelations.

"He would like for you to tell his wife, Jennie that whenever she's working in her garden and feels what she thinks is a spider web on her face, it's his way of saying hello. Tell her that he's around her all the time and that he will always love her."

Steve nods, promising to relay the highly personal message in full to the pilot's widow. When the dramatic session finally ends over an hour later, and before he exits Camp Ellis, Steve tells Michael Carpenter that he is convinced that righting this horrific wrong is a truly noble cause. He says he believes that the cause is so important, the Lord Himself is making an exception to the Biblical directive forbidding this type of spiritual contact. Steve asserts that he feels, without a doubt, that he is doing the right thing, acting on behalf of innocent, angelic beings, seeking only the truth and the highest good. Sharing the hidden truth about their crash with their families could not possibly be misguided or hazardous to anyone spiritually.

Why the Creator of the Universe would foster the miraculous survival of Ray's Bible and then ordain an exception to one of its principle written directives does not occur to him. He remains blindly committed to his cause, convinced that he is part of a very important crusade, seeking justice on behalf of fifteen heroic, egregiously dishonored men and their grieving families.

Four weeks later, Steve is at his residence in Atlanta, on the telephone with an aide to the Senior U.S. Senator from Georgia. The senator is a powerful member of the Senate Select Committee on Intelligence, and is responding to his request for help uncovering the truth, and seeking justice on behalf of the James Tyree Bomber Crew. He is optimistic that the senator's background as a World War II bomber pilot will ensure a natural desire in him to assist his brothers in arms and right this horrible wrong. The senator actually knew James Tyree's father quite well, during the elder Tyree's tenure with the Veterans of Foreign Wars in Washington, D.C. Senator Bancroft even delivered the eulogy for James Tyree's father on the floor of the United States Senate when Tyree's father died in 1963. The connection between the James Tyree family and the Senior U.S. Senator from Georgia was too good to bypass.

The senator's aide then informs him that the senator officially brought the matter of the James Tyree Bomber Crew to the senate floor in a closed session of the Senate Select Committee on Intelligence. High ranking Pentagon and Intelligence personnel were given one week to produce all the requested documentation, including an uncensored crash report. The senator's request was honored the following week and he was formally briefed in closed session by senior Pentagon and Intelligence officials regarding privileged information relevant to the James Tyree Bomber Crew.

The aide's unfolding summary has Steve anticipating the senator's full cooperation in his quest for justice on behalf of the James Tyree Bomber Crew. He is shocked and aghast when the aide ultimately relays the senator's heartless, cryptic conclusion.

"The senator is satisfied that you don't need to know what really happened to the James Tyree Bomber Crew."

"What?" he countered. "I'm not asking for the documents. I already have most of the basic information. I just want to know what the senator is going to do about this?"

"Based on what he learned from senior Pentagon and Intelligence officials, the senator has elected not to take any further action on the matter." the aide replied.

"Does he really expect me to tell that to James Tyree's widow and all the other families?" he snapped, his voice cracking with emotion.

"Tell them whatever you like, Mr. Lacey. The senator's position on this matter is firm."

In September 1999, Steve is on an airline layover in Richmond, Virginia, staring at the Richmond phone book in his hotel room. Having learned from James Tyree's widow, Jennie, that Tyree's good friend, A.J. Williams, another U.S. Eighth Air Force bomber pilot, might be located in Richmond, Virginia, he is elated to find him listed in the directory in front of him. There had been no contact between James Tyree's widow and A.J. Williams since the horrific crash, and Jennie Tyree had never really understood why.

Casually dialing the number, he hears a female voice on the other end and immediately asks to speak to A.J. Williams. The woman's cold, surly response catches him completely off guard.

"He died six months ago. Who are you and what do you want?" she snapped.

Desperate to recover the initiative, he begins offering a detailed explanation, certain his reason for calling would put the belligerent woman at ease. He was the nephew of one of James Tyree's crewmen and he was also a pilot investigating the crash. He felt certain that answer alone would be more than sufficient explanation to defuse her negative response and he could not have been more wrong.

"Do you want a piece of advice, mister?" she snarled after his initial explanation. "You'll never find out what happened to those men! My husband was there and saw the whole thing! They blew up right in front of him and you'll never find what you're looking for!" she taunted. "A.J. grieved for James Tyree for years. He used to sit up at night in his chair and cry endlessly for him until he finally died of a heart attack. He even tried to check into it himself and was ordered by the U.S. military to stop asking questions. You'll never find out anything, mister! I suggest you let it go!" she exclaimed. "Those were sad times and looking back at them won't do anybody any good!" she added, slamming the receiver down.

Obviously, Mrs. Williams somehow blamed James Tyree for her husband's death, even though he had outlived James Tyree by over forty years. She was undoubtedly well aware of U.S. Government sensitivity to the crash, but there was no way that her husband witnessed the bomber explode on the ground. She'd said with absolute certainty, "A.J. was taxiing past James Tyree's airplane when it suddenly exploded right in front of him!" Regardless of that gross misunderstanding, Williams widow wanted no part of this quest for justice. A follow up phone conversation by Tyree's widow, Jennie two days later produced virtually the same result, although the rejection she experienced was delivered in a considerably more civil tone.

One week later, Steve decides to clarify the Biblical directive of forbidden spiritual contact with the pastor of his local church. He and his wife Kay recently joined the large congregation, and although he didn't know the pastor personally, the man was highly regarded, and Steve believed a consultation on spiritual matters with such a scholarly figure might be beneficial. He also wanted to share the miraculous story of Ray's Bible with someone he felt could appreciate and perhaps interpret its religious significance.

Seated in the pastor's office for a 2 PM appointment, he is left to stare at the clock for the next forty-five minutes. Finally, the beleaguered pastor arrives, looking like a juggler with more balls in the air than hands to accommodate them.

"Sorry for the delay. I got caught in traffic on the way back from the bake sale." the pastor offered, shaking Steve's hand awkwardly.

"No problem." he replied, scrutinizing the pastor intently.

"It was really quite a bake sale. Mrs. McMahon always out does herself with that buttermilk pie of hers." the pastor declared, gesturing toward his full stomach.

"I'm sure." Steve replied, beginning to seriously wonder if he was in the wrong room.

"Well now, Steve, I know that you're new to the congregation and I can't tell you how glad we are that you chose us for your church family." the pastor continued. "I know you're a pilot and I must say that I really like your airline. Every time I've flown them they're always on time and they've never lost my luggage! Say … did you like the first friends we assigned both of you? They're really nice folks, aren't they?" the man stammered.

"Yes, very nice people." Steve echoed. "But I'm here about something else, something deeper, more spiritual."

"I see." the pastor replied. "What can I help you with?"

"Well, I was wondering if you could clarify the Biblical directive that specifically forbids spiritual contact with psychics and mediums?" he stated. "We have a situation in our family that involves regular spiritual interaction with the dearly departed."

"You aren't living in a haunted house, are you?" the pastor asked bluntly.

"No."

"Oh, thank God. I thought you were going to ask me to perform an exorcism on your home or your family." he exclaimed, removing a handkerchief and wiping beads of perspiration from his forehead.

"No, nothing like that. I just need to know if God occasionally makes an exception to his own written Biblical directives?" he asked pointedly.

"Maybe. Aren't there exceptions to almost everything?" the pastor replied.

"Yes, I guess so, but this is pretty weighty and I wanted the church's official position on exceptions to Biblical directives. Is anything ever important enough to warrant such an exception?" he asked directly.

"You know what they say … God answers everything either yes, no, or maybe. It sounds like you're in maybe territory." the pastor declared.

"I see."

"Now, will there be anything else? I have a wedding scheduled at 4 PM and I really need to get changed before all that gets started." the pastor declared.

"No, I guess that's it." Steve replied, rising to shake the pastor's hand. "Are you saying that it's not forbidden under every circumstance?"

"Maybe not. Let your heart lead you to what's right." the pastor declared, still brushing remnants of the bake sale from his shirt.

"Right." Steve managed, turning to leave.

"See you Sunday!" the pastor prompted, as Steve nodded with a smile, closed the door behind him, and shook his head in disappointment. Along his way to the parking lot he uttered,

"another doctor that couldn't cure a hangnail." as he walked purposefully toward his vehicle, eventually sliding into the driver's seat of the classic Ford pickup truck and starting the engine.

Ten days later, Steve has concluded that if he is going to uncover the truth and find justice for the Tyree Bomber Crew, he will have to do it unconventionally and more or less alone. With the exception of professional psychics and mediums, every agency or institution that he has contacted so far has either stonewalled, threatened, or proven to be totally useless. He is thoughtfully contemplating his lack of progress at this juncture in the investigation as he peruses Ray's Bible and feels its positive energy flow through him. On the table beside it is the faded letter to the Wilkins family from a Mr. Thomas, the Englishman that discovered Ray's Bible near the crash site. With no mailing address for the Wilkins family and uncertain how to return it, Mr. Thomas had elected to mail it to the church that initially distributed it to every serviceman from the Shelby, North Carolina area. Ultimately, the church forwarded Ray's Bible and the Thomas letter to the Wilkins family, where both were now in Steve's possession. Thomas letter stated that Ray's Bible was open to *John 3:16* when he discovered it several weeks after the crash. Steve pauses a moment to read the highlighted Biblical passage and to examine that particular page in Ray's Bible very intently. It showed no sign of exposure to external elements, even though it apparently lay exposed in the open countryside for several weeks after the crash. Ray's Bible actually appeared to be less weathered than the handwritten letter Thomas penned to the Wilkins family.

For God so loved the world that He gave His only begotten Son, that whosoever believe in Him shall not perish, but have everlasting life.
John 3:16

Steve contemplates the depth of such a sacrifice and the message Ray's Bible was trying to convey. He tries to correlate that heavenly message to the maddening experience he has endured in his quest to find justice for the Tyree Bomber Crew. In the turmoil and chaos, the hidden message regarding Ray's Bible remained lost in translation. He is convinced of one thing however ... that the divine intervention responsible for sheltering Ray's Bible and returning it to the Wilkins family, was also somehow nurturing an exception to the written Biblical directive against psychics, mediums and spirit communication. His commitment to act as an agent on behalf of the Tyree Bomber Crew remained unwavering, as he began making preparations for his upcoming trip to Black Hameldon, England, and the crash site of the Black Hameldon Bomber.

PART II

TUNNEL VISION

Chapter Four

Search and Discovery

"In covetousness, they will make merchandise of you."

2ⁿᵈ Peter 2:1-2

Three days later, Steve is en-route to Cambridge, England, filled with a mixture of anticipation and dread as he arrives at the Cambridge train station around mid-morning. Transitioning to a double deck bus for the final leg of his journey, he passes the time on the short bus ride reading Ray's Bible, before eventually disembarking at the entrance to the American Military Cemetery. He is filled with emotion as thousands of white cemetery crosses lining the property come into view. Exiting the bus and entering through the main receiving area, he pauses briefly at *The Wall of the Missing,* to stare at 5,125 names of American servicemen still missing in action from World War II. After a few minutes in reflection and prayer, he collects his thoughts and continues pursuing his immediate goal of locating the final resting place of the James Tyree Bomber Crew. Several more minutes pass as he strolls alone through the massive cemetery grounds, stopping to read each white marble cross before him, desperate to locate the Tyree Bomber Crew. Thirty additional minutes pass without success, until he suddenly notices the apparition of Uncle Ray standing all alone by a distant row of white crosses, motioning emphatically toward him.

He approaches the apparition of his late uncle a bit guardedly and notices that Uncle Ray is standing next to the grave of Eric Irving, the tail-gunner of the Tyree Bomber Crew. Uncle Ray smiles, greets him affectionately, and thanks him for coming, before openly declaring, "this isn't our place, but people still remember us here."

Gesturing at the white cross beside him, he then adds, "Eric will always be my friend. Death doesn't change that. We all have other things to do now, but we're together when we want to be. It's more like play time though now when we all get together."

Steve is caught off guard by the revelation and completely dumbfounded, unable to formulate an intelligent question as the window to another world lays open before him.

"This place is really for the families and the public. The Black Hameldon Bomber crash site belongs to my crew forever!" Uncle Ray said assertively. "You're always welcome there, of course. We couldn't do any of this without you. You're helping us with this very important matter, and you and I have been comrades of a different sort almost your entire life."

Steve nods awkwardly in response to his uncle's statement, still too overwhelmed for meaningful conversation.

"The privileged portions of the crash report that you are looking for will be made available to you at the crash site." Uncle Ray then stated bluntly. "Lieutenant Tyree wants to deliver the privileged portions of the crash report to you himself."

"I see." Steve uttered, trying to suppress any visible sign of apprehension at such an other-worldly invitation. "Can I ask you something, Uncle Ray?" he finally stammers.

"Yes, of course, Steve." Uncle Ray replied, still offering an uninterrupted smile.

"My wife and I have formally accepted Jesus Christ as our Lord and Savior." he said emphatically, withdrawing Ray's Bible from the small travel bag he was carrying with him. I owe a lot of my road to salvation to the study of your Bible. Your mother wanted me to have it when she learned about the relationship we've had since I was a child." Sensing sudden apprehension from Uncle Ray to the presence of his Bible, Steve pauses briefly before forcing himself to continue. "I was just wondering how all of this can be happening when the Bible, this miraculous little book of yours, specifically forbids such contact?"

Uncle Ray doesn't respond directly to the probing question and appears leery and reluctant to discuss the matter. Instead of providing an answer, he deflects attention by passing along a supposed third party greeting from Steve's deceased grandmother, including several intimate details regarding her recent passing. Moments later, Uncle Ray flashes a halfhearted smile and offers an abbreviated salute before disappearing from sight.

A short time later at the Lacey residence in Atlanta, Kay is home alone, with the exception of two sleeping dogs laying nearby. She is at the kitchen table paying bills when her attention is suddenly drawn to the sound of strange, mournful music playing upstairs. She forces herself to ignore the auditory intrusion as well as the inexplicable fact that it is emanating from Steve's unoccupied office. Instead, she channels her thoughts and energy into the earthly task before her, optimistic that the invasive activity will cease as suddenly as it began, if only she offers it no response. Her mental tug of war with the unexplained music continues for the next several minutes as it steadily increases in volume, until she finally completes the task before her, and with it the last bastion of mental distraction.

Devoid of busy work, she sits motionless, listening uneasily to the repetitive chorus of the song's heartsick melody. She recognizes it as a popular Glenn Miller song from the 1940's, but is unable to recall the title. What defies reasonable explanation is how the song can be emanating at high volume, playing over and over again in Steve's unoccupied office. Steve is in England, investigating the Black Hameldon Bomber crash and is not expected home for several more days. She has never heard this song before on his stereo and all the stereo equipment in his office was disconnected before he left for England. Under normal circumstances, the stereo must be manually activated by engaging the overhead light switch. The music only plays in conjunction with the overhead light, which is always illuminated when the stereo is operating. The stereo is also permanently tuned to a local top-forty FM radio station which does not play 1940's era music.

Eventually, reluctantly, she feels compelled to investigate the eerie, harmonic melody, and forces herself from the kitchen table. She prays that the activity will cease before she gets to the main staircase, a prayer that grows more fervent with each step she takes down the hallway leading to the stairs. Instead, the haunting, mournful sound grows progressively louder as she traverses the hallway and begins to approach the main staircase. Cautiously, she peers up the angled staircase, a vantage point offering only a restricted view of the hallway leading to Steve's office. There are no lights illuminated anywhere upstairs and she is well aware that it is not possible for the stereo to operate without light switch activation. Yet, the eerie, melodic refrain continues playing at high volume. Summoning all her courage, she places her right foot on the first step of the main staircase. Abruptly, her inner spirit emphatically warns her not to proceed any further.

Retreating from the staircase and carefully backing down the hallway, the eerie music suddenly and inexplicably stops. She listens attentively for several moments, but no sound at all is heard throughout the home. Days later, when the other-worldly experience is relayed to Steve, trial and error with a variety of 1940's era Glenn Miller music eventually identifies the song she was hearing. The actual significance of the song does not become apparent for several more days, when Steve relays the odd experience to James Tyree's widow, Jennie. From her, they learn together that Glenn Miller's *Moonlight Serenade* was the last song that Jennie and James Tyree danced to at the Officer's Club in Topeka, Kansas, the night before he was deployed overseas.

Later that same evening, electing to sleep on the downstairs couch until Steve returns from England, Kay is suddenly awakened by a menacing growl and the physical sensation of unseen hands trying to strangle her. Struggling to breathe, the violent attack escalates, and she is repeatedly assaulted by an evil presence that violently twists her neck and shoulders. Fighting for breath, she screams with everything her lungs can muster, an outcry that includes a rebuke in the name of Jesus of Nazareth. Instantly, the choking sensation and physical violence ceases, leaving her shaken, fearful, and feeling completely isolated, except for two rather bewildered German Shepherds.

Endeavoring for several minutes to calm the highly agitated dogs, her next thought is to warn Steve. He needs to know that something about the Black Hameldon Bomber crash and its crew is not right. He could be walking headlong into the middle of a demonic trap, at the hands of something that is pure evil. Glancing at the clock, she calculates the time zone difference to England and assesses that it's 9:30 in the morning there. Steve should be leaving Cambridge for the Black Hameldon Bomber crash site about this time. With the international calling card he left behind, she dials the Bed n' Breakfast in Cambridge. After a brief exchange, the female voice on the other end of the line politely reports, "Mr. Lacey checked out approximately twenty minutes ago."

Later that same day, Steve arrives in Black Hameldon, Moors area, England, and spends the entire day orienting himself and making preparations for his hike the next morning to the Black Hameldon Bomber crash site. When evening arrives, he begins scouring the village for an appropriate dining establishment and discovers his options are extremely limited. England isn't renowned for its culinary delights, and he is forced to settle on a traditional looking, working class establishment called the Damion Pub.

Inside, the century old local dive, the pub is filled with an odd assortment of inebriated patrons, crowded together in a smoke filled, poorly lit, noisy atmosphere that reminded him more of a sailor's bar than a dining establishment. He finds an open table in the corner of the pub's modest dining area and begins perusing the greasy, abbreviated menu, when a male waiter suddenly interjects. The barrel chested, gregarious man immediately pegs him as a "Yank" and begins making small talk concerning his reason for visiting the Black Hameldon area. Steve is tight lipped and aloof, but the waiter remains persistent to the point of becoming annoying.

"I must say mate, that leather coat of yours looks like an aviator's jacket. It could make some of this crowd uneasy, don't you know?" he stated bluntly.

"Why would that be?" Steve replied, downplaying the odd assertion from the waiter.

"Well, … it's the Black Hameldon Bomber … don't you know? It's an American bomber from the big war and they say it's crew manifests, none too happy, if anyone gets too close to their final resting place." the waiter offered, trying to sound as dramatic and mysterious as possible.

"Is that right?" Steve replied halfheartedly, trying unsuccessfully to dissuade the awkward conversation.

"Why … it's been a Moors area legend for fifty years!" the man declared proudly. "You look like a pilot in that leather jacket and you're obviously a "Yank" … maybe you're one of the Black Hameldon Bomber Crew, come to reek havoc on all of us this evening!"

"All right, you win. I admit it. I'm one of them." Steve said sarcastically. "Before we get too carried away though, what's your special this evening?" he asked, trying hard to change the uncomfortable subject.

"Shepherds pie." the waiter replied.

"I'll have that … and a pot of black coffee, please."

"Coming right up!?" the waiter replied, as he turned to leave.

After ordering, Steve begins surveying a Moors area map, straining to read its intricate topographical details in the pub's poor lighting, when suddenly a haggard local patron interrupts. The man is obviously well aware that Steve is an outsider to Black Hameldon, England and probably not just an ordinary tourist. He politely asks for permission to join him at the table and Steve agrees. The strange man is moving slowly, with a pronounced limp, as he takes a seat next to him, evidently recovering from several recent injuries. On closer inspection, Steve notices layers of bandages underneath the the man's outer garments. He also appears extremely troubled about something, pausing just long enough to introduce himself as Ian McShane and to offer Steve an awkward, albeit token handshake.

"Were you in some kind of accident?" Steve asks politely, as the strange man nods in response, but offers no details.

"How about you Yank … does your interest in the Moors area have anything to do with aviation?" he asks Steve pointedly in return.

"Well, sort of. I lost a relative in the Moors area." Steve replied, deliberately being vague and yet doing his best to avoid antagonizing the obviously distraught man.

Ian McShane remains unmoved and unrelenting, eyeing him with an incessant, semi-psychotic fixed stare. Wasting no time he then asks, "how long has your relative been missing?"

"Perhaps I misspoke." Steve replied. "My relative isn't missing. He's been deceased for quite some time."

Ian McShane continues pressing him for additional information, contrary to supposed British etiquette and cultural privacy standards.

"Was your relative lost in the big war?" he asks pointedly, staring at Steve and deliberately gauging his reaction. In response, Steve simply nods casually and pauses several moments before adding, "it was actually at the end of the big war in Europe."

Instead of avoiding antagonizing the man, the revelation of the timing of his late uncle's death seems to ignite a spark. Unable to contain himself emotionally, Ian McShane exclaims dramatically, "that's when the Black Hameldon Bomber crashed!"

Steve struggles to suppress any physical reaction to the supposed revelation, and innocently asks Ian McShane, "are you familiar with the details of the Black Hameldon Bomber crash?" In response, McShane becomes both defensive and intensely agitated. He is no longer able to keep his voice at a normal conversational level.

"I'm very familiar with it! That's where all my injuries occurred and it was no accident! Forget what these buzzards in the pub tell you! I didn't fall from the ridge overlooking the Black Hameldon Bomber crash! I was pushed, and then I was beaten by invisible, hellish beings that didn't want me there. Perhaps one of them was your relative!" he charged angrily, offering an icy stare.

Steve is dumbfounded by the strange assertion and stares at McShane in silence, pondering both his sanity and the validity of his far fetched statement. Ian McShane on the other hand, remains bolstered by several hours of heavy alcohol infusion as he continues challenging him unabated.

"You didn't come all the way from America just to collect the fifty pounds British Sterling reward! Was your relative on the Black Hameldon Bomber, or not?" he demanded, offering Steve a transfixed, emotionally disturbed stare.

Steve defers the loaded question and awkward stare down by asking for additional information …

"Tell me more about this reward you're referring to."

"Well … there has been a long standing dare in the area concerning the Black Hameldon Bomber. Anyone willing to hike alone to the crash site and produce a detailed photograph as evidence has always had bragging rights and a free drink waiting anywhere throughout the Moors area. A few weeks ago, a Scotsman stood right in this pub and added a fifty pounds British Sterling reward to that long standing dare. He taunted everyone in here, saying that they had dozens of American bomber crash sites in Scotland and that Scotsmen aren't afraid of them. He challenged us, if you will." McShane asserted, pausing momentarily to down another large alcoholic offering from the overly curious waiter.

Steve is silent, still reeling from the avalanche of odd experiences that he has had in the last twenty-four hours. He studies Ian McShane for quite some time before reluctantly admitting, "my relative was indeed on the Black Hameldon Bomber. He was the ball-turret gunner. I'm a professional pilot and I'm in the Moors area investigating the loss of the Black Hameldon Bomber. I'm here to learn the truth about what caused the crash."

In response to the heartfelt declaration, Ian McShane slams both his fists down forcefully on the small, wooden table and menacingly exclaims, "there is no truth to be found in that God awful place … no truth! The Black Hameldon Bomber crash site is a portal to hell and if you value your life you'd be well advised to stay away from it!"

Chapter Five

Myopia

"... because the darkness is disappearing and the true light is already shining."
John 2:8

The next morning, Steve is up early, on the heels of a restless night. His unsettling phone conversation with Kay, following his explosive interaction with Ian McShane at the Damion Pub made any hope of a good night's sleep elusive. He is now abundantly aware that he is being lured into something potentially quite dangerous, with little more than a ghostly invitation, predicated entirely on his implicit cooperation and decades of compliance. Electing to forego breakfast, he departs the Bed n' Breakfast at first light, avoiding potential onlookers and invasive questions from the local news media. Curiosity regarding his presence in Black Hameldon, England skyrocketed last night at the Damion Pub, culminating in a formal request for an interview by a local newspaper reporter.

Avoiding all contact with the news media and local residents as much as possible, he winds his way through the empty streets of Black Hameldon, managing to successfully pass through the entire village unnoticed. Eventually, he arrives at the entrance to the Warton Lodge, a local hunting and fishing lodge, and the official property owners of the Black Hameldon Bomber crash site, and surrounding acreage. As part of his hike preparations the day before, he formally secured permission to access Warton Lodge property and hike the trail to the crash site. In doing so, he was shown the lodge's detached laundry facility, which served as a temporary morgue and focal point of identification efforts following the horrific crash in 1945. The lodge manager confided in him that his staff won't work alone in the laundry facility to this day, and that they feel as if they are constantly being watched. The manager also stated that numerous guests over the years have reported ghastly, other-worldly experiences along the hiking trail and at the crash site itself. Those experiences included hearing disembodied voices shouting for help, bone chilling screams and menacing growls, witnessing lightning strikes out of a clear blue sky, and enduring sinister physical assaults resulting in cuts, bruises, and broken bones. He implored Steve to avoid attracting further attention to the crash site of the Black Hameldon Bomber, stating repeatedly that "it would only serve to hinder the lodge's business."

Donning his hiking gear, Steve skirts around the lodge's laundry facility and arrives at the base of the steep hiking trail leading to the crash site. The morning fog and pervasive dampness in the Moors area is greatly accentuating the gloomy nature of the task ahead. He is traveling light for this short daytime hike, with just simple rain gear, a canteen full of water, and Ray's Bible. He instinctively checks his watch before beginning the estimated forty-five minute climb to the Black Hameldon Bomber crash site. Almost immediately, he too begins to feel like he is being watched, but he tries to rationalize the eerie sensation. The poor visibility in the Moors area this morning is obviously not conducive to observing anything. He is meeting Uncle Ray, someone he has been in contact with almost all his life. And lastly ... he is no tourist or unwanted trespasser. He is working on behalf of the James Tyree Bomber Crew and he has an expressed invitation to the crash site. Uncle Ray and other members of the Tyree Bomber Crew are expecting him.

"What could go wrong?" he jokes uneasily.

At the first bend in the trail, he spots debris scattered over a wide area a few yards off to his right, and he leaves the trail to investigate. He quickly discovers that the debris is in fact used trauma kit packaging, and he concludes that this must be the location where rescuers found a seriously injured Ian McShane. He gathers some of the trauma kit packaging material and stows it in his small travel bag, making a mental note to ask Uncle Ray about the unfortunate incident, and Ian McShane's assertion of a violent, demonic assault.

Rejoining the hiking trail, he continues the steep ascent to the crash site. The remote nature and unnatural, eerie silence of the Moors area grow more apparent with each step he takes. There is absolutely no sign of life anywhere, not even insects. He begins to feel as though he is cocooned within a web of increasingly negative energy, a sensation that grows in intensity with every step. McShane's heated warning about the crash site being a portal to hell, paired with emotionally charged details regarding the attack that Kay experienced at home, resonate jointly in his mind. The ever present sensation that he could be walking headlong into a well planned demonic ambush dominates all his thought processes.

"Maybe I should have at least brought a camera along for the reward money." he joked.

The low visibility and dampness begin to improve dramatically as his elevation increases, and within minutes he is well above the thick layer of early morning ground fog. At what he perceives to be the halfway point on the trail, he pauses for a drink of water, and surveys the scene further up the trail. In the distance, high on an adjacent ridge, he spots a black ram frozen in position, eyeing him curiously. He surmises that the creature is well positioned to oversee the remaining portion of the hiking trail, as well as the crash site of the Black Hameldon Bomber just beyond the ridge ahead. The animal's fixed gaze has him feeling even more uneasy and vulnerable. He knows the domain he is entering is alien, surreal, and extremely hostile to intruders. With his survival instincts kicking in forcefully, he deliberately slows his pace to give all his senses a chance to elevate to their maximum. In response, he feels a steady adrenaline rush surging through his body. Against that adrenaline rush, he struggles to recall his Biblical studies, concerned that the overarching presence of a black ram could be a latent indicator of demonic activity.

Minutes later, as he approaches the crest dividing the trail from the crash site just beyond, he senses, but cannot see, an energy barrier across the trail abruptly divide, encouraging his entry as a disembodied voice exclaims … "welcome!" He does not respond to the gesture, but slows his pace and again surveys the trail ahead. He notices that it narrows considerably going forward, ideal landscape for an ambush attempt. Proceeding slowly and deliberately along the narrowing trail, he eventually reaches the crest overlooking the bomber's crash site. Surveying the scene directly below him, he is overwhelmed by the sight of such massive devastation. The Black Hameldon Bomber was obviously in a steep, vertical plunge on impact. It appears to have been completely out of control when the crash occurred. Scanning the highest ridge overlooking the crash site, he confirms the black ram's steady, uninterrupted gaze. The animal appears to be perplexed that anyone would approach its isolated domain. Its demeanor conveys an awareness that nobody is welcome here under normal circumstances and therefore all activity requires its steadfast attention.

As his focus returns to the wreckage of the ill fated bomber, Steve detects movement in the debris field directly below him. From his elevated vantage point, he sees a male figure in World War II military flying attire, standing in the middle of the debris field, apparently motioning toward him. Slowly descending the backside of the ridge in response, he is filled with trepidation as he approaches the figure cautiously. He wonders why anyone would be dressed like that and exploring this God forsaken place, especially today. Before he can utter a word, the entity greets him by name and openly declares, "it's good to see you again, Captain Lacey!"

Bewildered and speechless, Steve feels the fight or flight instinct kicking in even harder as the entity continues, "I have that privileged information you are looking for."

Before Steve can respond, the entity casually introduces himself.

"I'm Lieutenant James Tyree, command pilot of the Black Hameldon Bomber."

Steve is momentarily overwhelmed by the declaration and supernatural encounter, but he endeavors to remain as composed as possible. He stares for a moment at the man's face and recognizes him immediately as James Tyree from the crew photograph in his office. He instinctively tightens his grip on Ray's Bible for spiritual grounding, and manages to return a weak smile and nod as Lieutenant Tyree continues.

"My entire crew wanted to be here to share this special occasion with you."

In the blink of an eye, Steve is surrounded by the entire Tyree Bomber Crew and its six ill fated passengers. The faces of the crew are eerily familiar, and just like that night in the rain at Bradley International Airport, none of them has aged a day since the crew photograph was taken in 1944. Fifteen ghostly entities stare at him attentively, watching him in silence and gauging his reaction. Uncle Ray then interjects, extending his customary greeting, and like a good host, begins making formal introductions. One by one, Steve is introduced to the entire Tyree Bomber Crew and six passengers from that fateful day decades ago.

Following the lengthy introductions, the Tyree Bomber Crew and passengers immediately dispense with formalities and begin forming a tight circle around him. Without warning, they abruptly begin communicating their thoughts and experiences to him telepathically. The privileged portions of the accident report that he was told to expect to receive are abruptly imparted to him via a supernatural mental transference, as intimate knowledge and hidden details regarding the crash, that only they would know, begin to flow unrestricted. The transference process is designed to enable him to experience all the events surrounding the crash from each entity's perspective, including their mental and physical senses. Several minutes elapse, as the other-worldly, transference process unfolds to its horrific conclusion at 3:24 PM on June 13, 1945, the exact time of the bomber's crash.

Once the conclusion and aftermath are realized, Steve is suddenly transformed into a firsthand eyewitness to every detail, physical sensation, and nuance relevant to the bomber's final hours. The majority of the details are unsettling, a confirmation of what he learned from the psychic at Camp Ellis, and he is lost for words as he contemplates the travesty, betrayal, and potentially negative cultural impact to the revelation he just experienced. Undoubtedly, the details laid bare before him are powerful enough to rock the foundation of the U.S. Government if they were ever to become public knowledge.

He is dumbfounded and aghast, reeling from the horrific details of the graphic telepathic event, and the mental and physical aftermath of experiencing actual physical death. Speechless and overwhelmed, he stares at the fifteen entities in shock and dismay, trying to absorb the mysterious influx of information and collect himself emotionally. Lieutenant Tyree seizes upon his state of physical and mental vulnerability by injecting, "there's just one small change that needs to be addressed while we're all here together." he said flatly, as Steve stared at him in submissive silence.

"Instead of merely telling our families, we want this story told to the entire world, including how you received this privileged information and were able to solve the mystery of the crash. We want people to know and understand that there is real power available to them in the earthly domain, available to anyone if they will just call on it. All we ask for in return, is their service and absolute loyalty." Lieutenant Tyree said insistently, offering Steve a demanding, steadfast gaze.

Initially confused by the statement and still reeling from the transference process, Steve begins to slowly collect his thoughts. He eventually manages to ask Lieutenant Tyree for clarification and more specificity to his previous odd statement.

"To whom are you asking everyone to serve and for their absolute loyalty to be directed?" he asked carefully.

Unabashedly and without reservation, Lieutenant Tyree declares, "all service and all loyalty is to be reserved for and directed toward me and my crew."

Recoiling at the demonic declaration, Steve's spiritual discernment skills suddenly go into overdrive and he summons all his courage to ask, "what if people are not willing to offer you and the rest of the Black Hameldon Bomber Crew their service and absolute loyalty?"

Suddenly, a vile, overriding, disembodied voice, from the epitome of evil, Satan himself declares, "then they won't have any real power in my domain!"

Steve flinches in response to the precipitous, disembodied revelation of absolute satanic oversight, and instinctively thrusts Ray's Bible toward the apparition of his Uncle Ray.

"I challenge you, apparition of my Uncle Ray Wilkins, to hold your Bible again!" he shouted, as forcefully as he could, repeatedly thrusting the small Bible toward the apparition of Ray Wilkins.

The apparition of Ray Wilkins recoils and rejects any physical contact with the little book that had supernaturally survived dozens of combat missions and the crash of the Black Hameldon Bomber. Realizing there is no chance of the demonic entity's compliance, Steve slowly withdraws the small Bible and with it his direct challenge to the apparition. Instead, he immediately begins declaring aloud to Heaven his love and admiration for the real Tyree Bomber

Crew and labels the fifteen entities encircling him as satanic impostors before God. Kneeling in the debris field, while surrounded by an unholy whirlwind of darkness, he begins praying Holy Scriptures from Ray's Bible directly to his Father in Heaven. He implores the Lord to purify this evil, foreboding place and oversee his physical safety against the satanic forces that are encircling him. Drawing strength from the Word of the Lord, he reads aloud passage after passage unabated for the next several minutes.

When he finally concludes and pauses to scan the area around him, he realizes that he is now alone in the debris field of the Black Hameldon Bomber. There is no sign of the fifteen demonic entities or anything else for miles. Without hesitation, he turns to see if the menacing black ram is still gazing at him from the adjacent ridge, and he discovers that it too has abruptly vanished.

He thinks of Ian McShane and how right he was about this horrendous place being a portal to hell, but how wrong he had been about there being no truth here. In response to sudden soulful inspiration, he fosters a plan to ensure that truth and light always prevail in this soon to be sacred place, from this day forward. As part of that plan, he spends the next several minutes climbing to the vantage point vacated by the demonic black ram. Upon reaching the crest, he inserts Ray's Bible into a portion of the trauma kit packing material he was carrying, and places the items together at the optimum vantage point overlooking the crash site. He then repeats his prayer on behalf of the real Tyree Bomber Crew, his Uncle Ray, and for all the people that shall visit this sacred place in the future. He thanks his Heavenly Father for rescuing him from the satanic forces that encircled him and he implores his Father to one day make it possible for him to reunite with the spirits of the real Tyree Bomber Crew in Heaven.

When the task of strategically placing Ray's Bible and spiritually cleansing the area with prayer concludes, Steve begins a slow, prayerful trek back down the narrow hiking trail. As he does, he watches thick morning clouds give way to bright afternoon sunshine, and the gloomy, foreboding hiking trail transform into a well lit and easy to traverse pathway. The entire spiritual atmosphere of the crash site and surrounding area seems to have changed dramatically in a matter of minutes, with the ever present negative energy that was such a factor on the ascent, no longer apparent. He is also cognizant of the fact that the deafening, eerie silence of the Moors area has been replaced by a concert of nature in all directions.

At the mid-point of his descent, he stops to watch birds frolicking high overhead, and a white ram, ewe, and several young lambs grazing peacefully alongside the hiking trail. The arrogant, satanic utterance of the prince of darkness resonates once again in his mind as he resumes descending the trail.

"Then they won't have any real power in my domain! Then they won't have any real power in my domain!" he mimics, taunting the demonic forces that had duped him so successfully for most of his life.

Sensing a clear cut spiritual victory, his thoughts begin to shift to the Black Hameldon Bomber itself and the now resolved mystery. The hidden facts about the crash that he went to such extreme lengths to uncover, now seem almost inconsequential. The only revelation that he longs to share with the world is the unmistakable source of truth and light, the power of God's Word, not retribution for a man made tragedy. The power of God's Word was something his great-grandmother understood decades ago when she first handed him Ray's Bible. Now, he too fully understands that power and is committed to sharing his insight with anyone that will listen.

Twenty-five minutes later, the nagging question of whether a spiritual victory can be realized so quickly and decisively begins to gnaw at him. When he finally reaches the bottom of the hiking trail, he hesitantly approaches the laundry facility of the Warton Lodge and feels the same eerie sensation rising once more within him. At that moment, he concludes that total spiritual victory is unlikely to be realized in a single afternoon. The Bible is adamant that spiritual warfare is an ongoing battle as long as we inhabit an earthly, physical body. To that end, he begins to seriously ponder the potential time line and location of what he believes will be an inevitable demonic counter-attack.

Chapter Six

Reconstituted

"We use God's mighty weapons, not mere worldly weapons, to knock down the Devil's strongholds."   *2nd Corinthians 10:4*

On the long flight home, Steve feels more at ease in the coach section of the jetliner than he has anywhere else in days. Sleep is still elusive, but he no longer battles the incessant fight or flight instinct and its automatic sensory response. His victory over the forces of darkness at Black Hameldon, England was certainly decisive, but it left him emotionally drained, with his usual cockiness and bravado slow to rebound. At this juncture, he wonders if the biggest dilemma facing him in the short term is the privileged information that he retains in his subconscious memory regarding the Black Hameldon Bomber crash. The lifetime of spiritual deception and flagrant manipulation that he endured to solve the decades old mystery certainly did not undermine the accuracy of what he learned during the mental transference process. He knows in his heart that the Black Hameldon Bomber mystery is solved. The demonic hoard impersonated the Black Hameldon Bomber Crew in conjunction with their self serving, satanic master-plan, but beyond question, the fallen angels witnessed the tortuous events that led to the bomber's crash in 1945. He has no doubt that the information they shared with him at the crash site a few days ago was spot on.

Their deception and scheming were directed toward recruiting massive numbers of wayward followers. To them, solving the mystery was just a side show, a lure, a means to an end, to showcase the depth of their power in the earthly realm.

As the trans-Atlantic flight settles into the cruise portion, he begins to ponder the lifelong web of lies that eventually led him to this spiritual crossroad. Of all the outlets and entities he interacted with throughout this lengthy quest, only the families of the deceased crewmen, and the Illinois Society of Spiritualists and Naturalists at Camp Ellis provided any substantive, meaningful insight and reinforcement. Every other outlet, entity, or institution he encountered throughout this prolonged ordeal, either stonewalled, threatened, deceived, or was simply too incompetent to be worthwhile. After the transference process, he fully understands why authorities in the United States Government reacted to his initial inquiry the way they did. A murder investigation is an uncomfortable prospect at best, but even more so when you are the one ultimately responsible for the crime and the ongoing cover-up.

"We're satisfied that you don't need to know what really happened to the James Tyree Bomber Crew." he mimicked, as the gravity of the subject matter embedded in his subconscious memory ceaselessly invades his thoughts. With an evolving sense of priorities, he doesn't see those in the United States Government responsible for committing and covering up this heinous crime, as the principle antagonist. The adversary in his mind is more spiritual than earthly. It should not be surprising to anyone with adequate Biblical knowledge, that elements of the United States Government are actually under the control of satanic forces. The Bible clearly delineates that this world is the domain of the devil and that the majority of established bureaucracies around the world are evil, a la new Babylon. The lines in the spiritual battle between good and evil are clearly defined, and demonic forces have definite home court advantage. How to transpose the material embedded in his subconscious memory into something meaningful and enduring on behalf of the real Black Hameldon Bomber Crew still remains elusive. As an airline captain, he is expected to always have an answer at the ready, never to be without some kind of a plan. Sliding his seat all the way back and closing his eyes, he considers that degree of certainty to be polar opposite to the confusing reality of the spiritual dogfight at hand. For the next several minutes, he ponders the complex, unearthly puzzle he has inadvertently inherited, before exhaustion eventually overtakes him and he surrenders to much needed sleep.

He is awakened some time later by activity in the aisle next to him, as the flight attendants conduct the coach class meal service. Glancing at his watch, he realizes that he has been asleep almost two hours. As the fog of sleep slowly retreats, embedded images of the Black Hameldon Bomber immediately resurrect, and he resumes pondering the dilemma of a suitable course of action. It seems every waking moment since he left Black Hameldon, England has been consumed with finding an elusive solution to an ethereal puzzle, one that properly addresses his quandary from an eternal, Godly perspective. It's not easy to rebound from the sudden realization that your presumed guardian angel is actually a demonic imitator committed to your ultimate destruction. Without the presence of Ray Wilkins however, he feels unsupported and suddenly quite vulnerable. Someone he thought was protecting him his entire life is no longer in that role, and he realizes how dependent he had become on that counterfeit entity. He is also concerned that the thin line between love and hate might expose him to serious retribution, and Ray Wilkins could become a threat to his welfare. Their lifetime relationship was predicated entirely on his gullibility, and outright acceptance of his role in an intricate, demonic scheme of mass deception.

Scanning his watch again, he calculates that with slightly more than four hours remaining, they must be near mid-ocean. The seat next to him is not occupied and none of the crew working the flight has recognized him, leaving the door to twenty questions about his visit to England firmly closed and locked. His phone conversation with Kay, before departing England, left him perplexed and skeptical regarding whether his spiritual victory was indeed decisive. Solving the mystery of the crash and sterilizing the crash site, didn't seem to have lowered the level of spiritual activity at the Lacey residence.

Wouldn't those God forsaken television shows that purport to investigate and analyze spirit activity have a field day at the Lacey residence? For that matter, wouldn't his employer be aghast at that kind of publicity involving one of its captains? He shudders at the thought of such a circus of ignorance and concludes unilaterally that there is no reservoir of spiritual insight and sanity aside from the Word of God. From his conversation with Kay, he begins to realize that winning a spiritual battle is going to be quite different than winning a spiritual war. His embedded memories regarding the Black Hameldon Bomber represent a high stakes moral dilemma, but the threat of future spiritual conflict with over a dozen enraged satanic beings remains a very real threat in the short term.

His attention is suddenly drawn to activity in the aisle next to him. What appears to be an ordinary, male passenger brushes past him hurriedly, seemingly heading for the mid-cabin lavatory a few steps beyond. At the lavatory door, the passenger stops, turns and glares menacingly at him. Meeting the stranger's gaze, he suddenly realizes that he is staring into the sunken, haunting eyes of James Tyree, the apparition of the Black Hameldon Bomber's command pilot. Steve's concern for what might await him upon arrival in Atlanta is now pushed to the back burner. Demonic impersonators of the Black Hameldon Bomber Crew are aboard his home bound jetliner and they are not feigning any kind of camaraderie or forgiveness.

He returns the entity's menacing gaze for several seconds, and deliberately stifles his reaction as James Tyree's eyes transition to a deep, glowing red. The ominous figure then enters the aircraft lavatory and closes the door behind him. Steve is transfixed on the lavatory door for the next several minutes, but there is no sign of any movement. Then, he watches in horror as a mother and child approach the mid-cabin lavatory from the opposite direction. He can only imagine what evil awaits such innocence within the confined aircraft lavatory compartment. Desperate to protect the innocent, he is on the verge of physically throwing himself into the lavatory ahead of them, and is therefore dumbfounded when the mother and child nonchalantly enter the aircraft lavatory and exit with no apparent concern a few minutes later. He has a spiritual epiphany at that very moment, 33,000 feet above the middle of the Atlantic Ocean. He realizes that his spiritual battle is obviously far from over, and that the battle will be fought mostly in his mind. If he can take his own thoughts captive, as the Apostle Paul suggested, the power of the dark side will be greatly diminished.

The timing of his epiphany is crucial, for in the blink of an eye, the unoccupied seat next to him is filled with a tearful, little girl, holding a teddy bear and asking mournfully, "do you know where my mommy is?"
He observes the little girl without comment, carefully assessing her dubious legitimacy, before committing to any kind of a response.

"I don't know you or your mommy." he replies sternly. "Perhaps the father of lies is your father too." he charges, watching the little girl's eyes turn fiery red as her voice changes to a low pitched, menacing snarl.

"What's the matter Lacey? You aren't afraid of a little girl are you?" the satanic voice taunted, as the figure of the little girl gnashed its teeth violently and offered him an inhuman, unearthly sneer, before abruptly vanishing from sight.

"This is going to be a long four hours." he said sarcastically, peering guardedly in all directions. "I'd really hate to see any of this get back to the crew room. I'll be the talk of the airline."

"Are you interested in a meal, sir?" one of the flight attendants interjected, temporarily suspending his mental jousting with the spirit world.

"Sure. Why not?" he replied, smiling halfheartedly and lowering his tray table in response. The normally unappealing airline food looked downright palatable after the English fare he had endured for the last few days. Based on previous experience, normality also seemed to be an important weapon in the arsenal during periods of spiritual conflict. "In abnormal times, do normal things." he stated philosophically, readying himself to eat.

Just as he is about to begin the meal, his action is interrupted by a deep, booming voice over his right shoulder.

"Hey ... Steve Lacey! I thought that was you! You aren't really going to eat that airline bilge are you son?" the voice cajoled. "I thought I trained you better than that."

"Bob Swanson?" he exclaimed dumbfounded, as his long time mentor dropped heavily into the empty seat beside him.

"What on Earth are you doing here?" Swanson asked inquisitively. "Do you have family or business in England?"

Steve does not respond, but stares at the man coolly in detached silence, scrutinizing him in intricate detail and critically assessing his legitimacy.

"What's the matter, Steve? You act like you've seen a ghost! Don't you remember me? " Swanson asked. "You aren't too good for your old buddy now that you have a captain bid on the heavy iron are you?"

"No." Steve replied, stoically.

"Well, what is it old buddy? Cat got your tongue?" Swanson teased.

"Not exactly. It's just that I remember being a pall bearer at your funeral two years ago." he replied bluntly, watching the would be impostor snarl as it hissed savagely, in like fashion to the little girl, before also abruptly vanishing.

"Is anybody on here real?" he asked rhetorically.

"I'm real." the lady across the aisle declared, smiling seductively at him.

"Congratulations." he replied, ignoring the strange, flirtatious woman as he carefully surveyed the other inhabitants of the aircraft's coach section.

"What exactly are you looking for?" she persisted. "Maybe I can help you find it."

"I don't think so." he said dismissively. "I know exactly what I'm looking for and where I can find it."

"Then perhaps we should just start with an introduction. My name is Nora."

"Really?" he replied sarcastically.

"Why is that so hard to believe?" she asked with contrived innocence.

"It's a long story with a sad ending." he replied, deliberately remaining dismissive and aloof.

"We don't land for at least three more hours. I'd love to hear it if you'd like to share it with me." she suggested.

"It's not for public consumption … sorry." he replied, continually scanning the coach class cabin for anything out of the ordinary.

"That's too bad. May I ask you just one thing before I leave you alone? Do you know anyone killed in a fire?" she inquired with a wicked, psychotic grin, as he watched her eyes redden and her face contort to a repulsive death mask.

In response, he steels himself to avoid appearing unnerved, even though this time, the entity does not retreat, but remains seated directly across the aisle from him, offering an unwavering, psychotic grin, and demonic gaze.

"What's your end game here?" he demanded. "I'll never do whatever you and your friends want me to do."

"Never is a long time." the female entity growled.

"You'll probably spend it staring at me. What is it you freaks want? A fight? Don't you have anything better to do?" he taunted.

"No … this is what we do. You seem to forget …we had an agreement. We gave you what you wanted, but you didn't give us what we wanted. Now, we want what we gave you back." the entity declared emphatically.

"And just how are we going to arrange that?" he demanded, glaring at the female entity with a *High Noon* stare.

"The mental transference process works both ways." the entity said flatly. "With us all together again, we could easily take back what we gave you. If not, perhaps we could just take you out!"

"Forget it." he declared. "You lied and manipulated me for years! I owe you nothing! Maybe I can't rock your world, but I know someone that can. I rebuke all of you in the name of Jesus of Nazareth! In His holy name, I demand that all of you vacate this airplane immediately! Get behind me Satan!"

Instantly, the seat occupied by the demonic female entity is emptied as Steve watches her disappear. He then pauses for several seconds to catch his breath, lower his pulse rate, and carefully assess the spiritual battlefield.

"They want their money back. Well, the Lacey's don't give refunds!" he snarled, eyeing the airline meal before him and contemplating his next move. The meal looked cold, dry, and utterly inedible, perfect sustenance for the strangest airline flight of his entire life. "Thank you, Father for the blessing of this meal." he prayed, before directing his attention to the meal offering in front of him. "And thank you for protecting me from all the things in this world that are opposed to your will and your way. Amen!"

For the next three hours, he checks his watch repeatedly, trying to gauge how much longer this in-flight torture will continue. He has already calculated that the aircraft coasted in over an hour ago at what looked like Wilmington, North Carolina, and he is anticipating their descent into Atlanta, beginning any minute. In spite of the unearthly distractions, he managed to successfully complete the mundane task of filling out the U.S. Customs form in front of him. He is anxious to claim his luggage and clear customs as quickly as possible. Kay is supposed to be picking him up at curbside and they have a lot to discuss. She's really been patient, considering the nature of everything that's been thrust on her. He is also convinced that the Lacey household is now being targeted for revenge, and he knows that the two of them need to develop and implement a defensive strategy for the upcoming spiritual battle on the home front.

Forty-five minutes later, he is progressing nicely toward his task of clearing U.S. Customs. After retrieving his luggage in record time, he is nearing the end of the lengthy customs process at the Atlanta International Airport.

"Was the purpose of your visit business or pleasure, Mr. Lacey?" the U.S. Customs officer inquired.

"Family business." he responded. "No commerce."

"I see. Do you have relatives in England?" the U.S. Customs officer continued.

"No. I was honoring a World War II casualty, my uncle."

"I see … welcome home Mr. Lacey!" the U.S. Customs officer declared with a professional smile. "Next in line!"

Steve nods and begins the long trek to the front of the International Terminal. He glances at his watch and realizes that the original time estimate he gave Kay was pretty close and that she should be waiting at curbside for him. He dials her cell phone to confirm that she is nearby and Kay answers on the third ring.

"Hello?"

"Hi, honey. It's me."

"Where are you?" she asks curiously.

"At the International Terminal. I just cleared customs." he replied.

"Oh … we have a problem. The parking in front of the International Terminal is blocked. I had to park in front of Terminal A." she said hesitantly.

"Uh-oh." he replied. "I'm dragging all this luggage and that means I'll have to ride the tram."

"Can you get someone to help you carry it?" she suggested.

"It isn't the luggage. That just slows me down. The problem is the tram. It's pretty isolated down there and not that well lit." he stated.

"Are you worried about muggers?" she asked startled.

"No. I'm worried about something much worse. I'll tell you all about it when I get there. Stay put! I'm coming to you!" he ordered, before hanging up his cell phone.

Minutes later, Steve is on the down escalator to the inter-terminal tram and he is relieved to find the area crowded with fellow travelers. Strength in numbers, he tells himself as the escalator deposits him on the lower tram level. Within minutes the opposite direction tram arrives and the majority of the people waiting clamor aboard. Watching it disappear down the stretch of rail in the opposite direction, he suddenly realizes that he has become much more isolated in the tram waiting area. There is no sign of the tram to Terminal A as he carefully studies the faces around him. Only then does he realize that one of those faces is also engrossed in studying him.

When their gazes meet, he recognizes the apparition of Cole Johnson, co-pilot of the Tyree Bomber Crew. The counterfeit specter makes no attempt to approach, but offers him an unblinking stare, in an obvious, egregious attempt at psychological and spiritual intimidation. Having formally met only days before under entirely different surroundings and circumstances, their current hostile encounter resembles two entities posturing for mortal combat. Much had changed in the last few days, and the message being conveyed by Satan's surrogate this time was all out warfare.

The arrival of the Terminal A tram was a welcome sight as Steve's eyes dart back and forth from the track to the ominous entity gazing at him. Gathering his luggage, he eases through the tram's doorway, momentarily losing sight of the stalking entity in the process. The Terminal A tram is nearly filled to capacity as he burrows aboard, trying to distance himself from the pursuing entity. He immediately searches the faces of everyone around him on the tram, trying to assess other potential threats. None are familiar. His eyes then automatically sweep the crowd further out. Only then does he see him. There is no mistaking that face, no chance of casually overlooking him in a crowded airport tram. Twenty steps away, hidden behind a gaggle of travelers, Ray Wilkins, absent his normal disarming smile, is fixated on him. The apparition's eyes are empty and cold this time, and instead of conveying love and acceptance, he is watching Steve like a stalking animal beholding prey.

"Do you want your Bible back?" Steve taunted, matching Ray Wilkins fixed stare, and refusing to show the entity any hint of fear. "I don't have it, but I picked this one up in duty free." he cajoled, retrieving a small, King James Bible from his travel bag and openly daring the entity to respond. Ray Wilkins retreats a half step, but continues staring menacingly at him as the tram slowly rumbles along the dimly lit corridor toward Terminal A.

After what seems like an eternity, the tram finally slows to a stop in the lower level of Terminal A. The doors open and dozens of travelers depart in unison, heading for the up escalator to the ground level of the terminal building. Burdened with both checked and carry on luggage, he struggles to keep pace and avoid being left behind. Reaching the escalator, he discovers that among the group of hurried travelers on the escalator with him, he is sandwiched between Ray Wilkins ahead of him, and Cole Johnson behind him. He then recalls his epiphany aboard the airplane at mid-ocean, that the battlefield in this struggle is mostly in his mind, and that he must take every thought captive. Grasping his new duty free Bible, he closes his eyes and asks his Creator for heavenly protection and spiritual strength in the battle with pure evil that surrounds him. When he opens his eyes, expecting an outright physical confrontation, both entities have vanished, there is no imminent confrontation, and for the moment no further trace of the skulking demons.

"Lucky for them. I was just starting to get mad." he joked, carefully scanning the environment around him.

Seconds later, the escalator deposits him on the ground level of Terminal A, and the bright sunlight streaming through the curbside windows provides welcome relief. He strolls outside, near curbside check in, but Kay is nowhere in sight. Anxious to keep moving, he dials her cell phone and she answers on the second ring.

"Where are you? I'm here at Terminal A." he declared, still automatically searching the faces of everyone passing by.

"A cop made me move." Kay stated. "I'm circling back around to the entrance. I should be there in two minutes."

"I'll be the good looking one out front." he joked. "See you when you get here."

Immediately after hanging up, his cell phone rings. Thinking it must be Kay, he doesn't check the caller ID.

"I'm still here." he declared sarcastically.

"Hello? Is this Mr. Lacey, Mr. Steve Lacey?" the caller asked insistently.

"Yes. What can I do for you?" he replied.

"This is Brandon Winston, senior aid to Senator Bancroft. How are you today Mr. Lacey?"

"Why? Are you taking a survey?" he retorted.

"Oh, no sir. I'm calling on behalf of Senator Bancroft. He would like to schedule a meeting with you to discuss your recent trip to England." the aid announced mechanically.

"Is he tracking me? Steve said accusingly.

"Oh, no sir. The senator received a call from our Intelligence officials in Washington, D.C. Apparently they received a call from their British counterparts at MI5."

"Uh-huh."

"Well, Mr. Lacey. Senator Bancroft was asked by our Intelligence officials to debrief you regarding your trip. When would be a convenient time for you?" the aid asked bluntly.

"How about half past never?" he replied sharply.

"Sir?"

"You may inform Senator Bancroft that I'm satisfied he doesn't need to know what really happened to the James Tyree Bomber Crew." he snapped. "And I would also appreciate it if you would lose my number. Goodbye …"

He is still grinning seconds later when Kay pulls up in front of the terminal in his classic Ford pickup truck.

"I thought you didn't like driving my truck." he teased, climbing into the right seat and exchanging a kiss with Kay.

"You sure are in a good mood considering." she stated.

"Yes I am. I just got off the phone with Senator Bancroft's office."

"Why on Earth would you call him?" she asked startled.

"I didn't call him. Suddenly, he wants to talk to me." he replied with a smirk.

"Are you going to listen to what he has to say?" Kay asked curiously.

"No, but I imagine he's involved in a lot of screaming and hair pulling right now."

"You didn't." she said, eyeing him accusingly.

"Oh, yes I did! Now, it's his turn to sweat." he stated emphatically, as Kay steered the Ford pickup truck toward the airport exit.

PART III

SPIRITUAL LEGACY

Chapter Seven

Encore

"Destruction is certain for those that say evil is good and good is evil."

Isaiah 5:20

When the Lacey's finally arrive home, they are unable to enter. Two black Suburbans, with U.S. Government license plates, are parked at their residence, one in the middle of the driveway and the other at the front, curbside. As Steve peers through the front windshield of the vehicle at the curb, it appears to be occupied by several men, and judging by their reaction to the Lacey's arrival, they've been waiting quite awhile.

"Well, it looks like the senator got my message." Steve said sarcastically, flashing a mischievous grin at Kay.

"What do you want me to do?" she asked excitedly, as if seriously contemplating a hasty retreat.

"Relax …" he implored, grasping her knee for emphasis. "This is nothing compared to what I've just been through. Follow my lead and let me do all the talking." he instructed, as Kay carefully parked the Ford pickup near the front curb and shut off the engine.

Immediately, doors opened in both Suburbans, and a half dozen intense looking men approached the Lacey vehicle, dividing into two groups at the last moment to cover both sides of the truck.

"Are you Steve Lacey?" the lead agent asked.

"No. We're Bonnie and Clyde." Steve replied.

The humorless, and now semi-irritated man stared at both of them intently, and then slowly repeated the question. "Are you Steve Lacey?"

"Okay, you got me. I'm Steve Lacey. This is my wife, Kay. What can we do for you?" he replied, nonchalantly.

"I'm Agent Prentice, Defense Intelligence Agency." the man declared, flashing U.S. Government credentials. "Senator Bancroft needs to debrief you regarding your trip immediately. We have been instructed to escort you to his office."

"Do we have a choice?" Steve asked sarcastically.

"No, sir. We were ordered by the senator to escort both of you immediately."

"Are we under arrest?" Steve asked, still trying to sound casual.

"No, sir. You're under escort." the agent replied, as the group of DIA agents ushered Steve and Kay toward one of the awaiting Suburbans.

Forty-five minutes later, the Lacey's arrive in the parking garage of a large corporate office complex in downtown Atlanta, and are hastily shown to the office of the Senior Senator from Georgia. Twenty-five minutes elapse, in awkward silence, until the government imposed detention is interrupted by a single agent responding to a radio message in his ear piece. After listening intently for a moment, he cryptically declares, "Senator Bancroft is three minutes out."

Steve nods and sarcastically proclaims, "I hope I can stay awake that long. It was a long ride home from London."

The agent, sporting a crew cut that denoted ex-marine, is unresponsive, and resumes an uninterrupted, poker faced stare at an imaginary point in open space. The scene is surreal and stereotypical, but Steve is too tired to exploit it for comic relief. He looks at his watch and tries to calculate the length of time it's been since he had a decent night's sleep. His mind and body feel like they just flew a West Coast red eye and then ran a marathon. He passes the remainder of the government imposed time out reflecting on the negative effect of sleep deprivation, until his drifting thoughts are interrupted by a door opening, voices resounding, and a portly man with a shock of gray hair entering the room.

"Captain Lacey? I'm Senator Bancroft." the self-important figure declared, offering a weak politician's handshake. "And you must be Mrs. Lacey ... may I call you Kay?" he asked, feigning sincerity and extending a second handshake toward Kay.

"Yes, of course." she replied, returning the warm buttermilk handshake, but ever-conscious of the fact that this was the man responsible for having them both involuntarily summoned to downtown Atlanta.

"Do you mind telling me why we're here?" Steve interrupts, openly contesting the involuntary nature of the impromptu meeting and all the contrived politeness.

"Certainly. Be seated and we'll get right to it. I know you must be exhausted after that long flight." the senator suggested, probing for common ground.

"Couldn't this have waited a day or two?" Steve demanded, eyeing the senator suspiciously.

"Well, Captain Lacey, I ask you to bear with us. This is a matter of very high level national security, and it's important that we understand exactly what you learned on your trip to England. This meeting is an opportunity for you to share with us everything you learned about the Black Hameldon Bomber crash." the senator proclaimed, eyeing Steve warily but also probing for the slightest hint of any uncertainty.

"An opportunity? Like I'm supposed to seize the moment?" Steve exclaimed.

"You could say that ... " the senator replied awkwardly.

"Well, senator ... I believe you already know what happened to the Black Hameldon Bomber and exactly why it crashed. This is just a fishing expedition to see if your fifty year old cover story is still intact. You know what happened to those men and you also know that its shameful, a travesty of justice, and the epitome of betrayal. We both know they deserved a lot better." he decreed, before adding … "And you also know that the United States Government got away with it!"

"I see." the senator said, visibly recoiling at the scathing assessment.

"Now, here's the weird part, senator. As culpable as the United States Government and Office of Strategic Services are in all of this, I'm just not that interested in that aspect of it. I'm contending with something much more sinister than an agency of the United States Government. You see, senator, I'm in the middle of a spiritual battle." he stated firmly, offering the senator an unblinking, icy stare, and daring him to say something inappropriate.

"A spiritual battle you say …?" the senator echoed, suppressing his reaction to the strange declaration and trying desperately to avoid the appearance of mocking.

"I don't expect you to understand or appreciate such things, senator. Most people are ignorant when it comes to spiritual matters. Rest assured however, that I know everything you know about the Black Hameldon Bomber crash and a lot more. I know that those responsible for it in the U.S. Government got away with murder. The people in power always get away with murder, at least on this side of the veil. Justice for all of you will only come when God judges everyone for what they've done during their time on Earth. You have no reason to fear what I might say or do, senator, but you should be absolutely terrified that you'll have no answer for God on judgment day." he declared, watching the unsettling pronouncement fall heavily on the senator.

"Now, see hear a minute …" the senator stammered, reeling at the thought of impending judgment and corresponding punishment by the Supreme Being of the universe.

"Take it easy, senator. You're still in charge. It's just that I don't see the Black Hameldon Bomber crash as a national security issue, like you do. I see it as just another element of the struggle between good and evil. You, and the people you represent are evil, and if you don't change your ways all of you are destined to experience a satanic landlord throughout eternity." he exclaimed. "Now, unless you're going to arrest us, I'd like to get some sleep before your future landlord returns for an encore."

"Aren't Christians supposed to love people and care about their souls and where they spend eternity?" the senator chided, trying to recover lost momentum.

"Indeed, and only God Almighty can truly read someone's heart, senator, but the rest of us can perceive the clues of a hardened heart, and your heart could crack walnuts. There appears to be no humanity in any of you people. None of you seem to be righteously indignant, or have your sensibilities even slightly offended by the fact that fifteen brave men were murdered on their way home after saving the world. Scripture tells us that "*you will know them by their works,*" and your only concern at this late date is whether or not your cover story will still fly! Therefore, you senator, are beyond my help." he stated emphatically, rising to leave.

"Not so fast, Captain!" the senator exclaimed. "We aren't finished yet!"

"Now what?" Steve demanded.

"Would you be willing to sign a nondisclosure agreement regarding the Black Hameldon Bomber crash?" the senator asked flatly. "It's standard procedure for any American citizen handling classified information."

"You have to be kidding!" Steve retorted. "I haven't handled any classified information! I learned the truth from your future landlord! Besides … who would I tell? The news media? Their approval rating is in the gutter with yours!" he taunted. "I told you this is a spiritual battle, senator. You and your ego just don't get it. You're a bit player, a side show in all of this."

After an awkward silence, the senator ominously declared, "keep in mind that we have ways of getting what we need. I'm sure the last thing someone in your position needs is trouble with the IRS or perhaps the FAA? You understand me, don't you, Captain?"

"Better than you seem to understand me." Steve replied. "You're just adding to the list of things you'll have no answer for on judgment day."

"Very well, Captain. Thank you for taking the time to discuss this matter with us. I'm glad we were able to come to a mutual understanding that assures your cooperation." the senator said mechanically.

"Uh-huh."

"Take Mr. and Mrs. Lacey home, Agent Prentice. I've got a few phone calls to make." the senator directed. "I'll be here waiting when you get back." he added, offering a halfhearted, departing handshake to Steve and Kay as they rose to leave.

"Good luck with your spiritual battle, Captain." the senator said with mildly suppressed sarcasm.

"And good luck with yours, senator. You should know that the first step in winning a spiritual battle is recognizing the fact that you're in one." he stated flatly, before abruptly turning to exit the senator's office.

Less than an hour later, Steve and Kay are back at their residence, temporarily unshackled from governmental third party interference. Steve jumps into his classic Ford pickup, starts the engine, and carefully pulls the truck into the garage. Waiting outside, Kay unlocks the back door to the home, but pauses in the doorway, hesitant to enter.

"What's the matter?" he asks curiously, after securing the truck and exiting the garage.

"Nothing. I just need a big, strong, handsome man with me before I go in." she replied coyly.

"Really? How long before he gets here?" he quipped.

"Oh, he's here now." Kay giggled, motioning for him to enter first.

As he enters the home through the back door, he is welcomed by two very excited German Shepherds. Everything appears normal, with the exception of the answering machine on the built-in kitchen desk, which is repeatedly flashing the number twelve.

"Wow! We're really popular all of a sudden!" he exclaimed, rewinding the tape and listening to a diatribe of incoming messages as Kay simultaneously unloads dirty laundry from his suitcase into the adjacent laundry room. Most of the messages are from Senator Bancroft's office, appealing for an urgent meeting in the interest of national security. Two are from family members of the Tyree Bomber Crew, including James Tyree's widow, Jennie, soliciting updates on his trip to England. Those would be particularly difficult calls to make he realized, as Kay continued emptying the contents of his suitcase. Near the end of the lengthy playback, he paused to listen to the voice of a female secretary at one of the large seminaries in the Atlanta Metro area, offering to schedule a meeting with one of the seminary's prominent theologians. Apparently, the senior pastor of Lacey's church solicited additional assistance on his behalf after their abbreviated and decidedly inconclusive meeting weeks ago.

"That sounds somewhat promising." he said, replaying the message a second time for clarity.

"You really should talk to him. He might have personal experience with this sort of thing." Kay suggested.

"I would certainly hope so. Well … I guess we can give organized religion another chance. Maybe they were just having an off day the last time." he surmised, as he slowly and deliberately glanced around the room for anything unusual or out of place.

"And to their credit … organized religion hasn't conspired to kill a deity in over 2000 years!" Kay joked.

"Yep, they're definitely on a winning streak!" he said sarcastically, still glancing around. "I don't see anything amiss down here." he added, moving cautiously throughout the downstairs.

"Uh-huh. Maybe my hero scared them off." she replied, offering him an encouraging smile.

"Maybe they're just reloading." he joked, peering carefully into every downstairs room before finally heading upstairs to his office.

Reaching the base of the main staircase, he directed, "come with me!" as he led the way upstairs, with Kay following close behind.

At the door to his office, he cautiously turned on the overhead light, which appeared to be working normally. Then, walking slowly to the other side of his office, he confirmed that the stereo was indeed unplugged, before plugging it back into the wall socket. Instantly, tuned to a local top-forty FM radio station, the stereo began playing *Piano Man* by Billy Joel.

"Not exactly nostalgia music from the forties." he declared, glancing around his office, searching intently for anything out of place.

"Well … that's odd."

"What's odd?" she asked curiously.

"The clock wasn't unplugged and yet it's stopped at 3:24. So is the wristwatch I left on my desk. Every timepiece in this room is stopped at 3:24."

"Wouldn't that make sense if the power went off?" she suggested.

"They each have independent power sources, so I won't oversleep in case of a power failure. Even my travel alarm clocks are stopped at 3:24." he added, eyeing the miniature travel alarm clocks curiously.

"I don't remember a power failure while you were gone." she stated. "None of the clocks downstairs are stopped, just in here."

"Want to know something else that's a little off the deep end?" he said ominously.

"What?"

"According to the crash report, the Black Hameldon Bomber impacted the ground at exactly 3:24. Every timepiece I discovered at the crash site was stopped at 3:24."

"Anywhere else, that would sound strange, but around here, it sounds like just another day." she said with deadpan humor, squeezing his hand reassuringly. "I'm really glad you're home."

"Me too. But I wonder if we're really alone or if I'm still being watched all the time like I was at the crash site? I'm too tired to entertain the dark side this evening. Part of me doesn't know what time zone it's in. If I don't lay down soon, I'm going to fall down."

Several hours later, the pair is abruptly awakened by a loud crashing sound down the upstairs hallway. Sensing a potential threat from an intruder, Steve grabs the 12 Gauge shotgun stowed under the bed, and begins moving cautiously toward the source of the sound.

"Careful!"she demanded.

"Be quiet! Stay here, so I know exactly where you are!" he directed, pausing to listen attentively for several seconds before carefully easing forward into the hallway. Kay is speechless, unable to respond as she watches Steve disappear into the darkness. Seconds pass, and her apprehension grows exponentially, until she eventually hears him calling her name from down the hall …

"Kay! Come take a look at this!"

Following the sound of his voice toward a light down the hallway, Kay finds him in the spare bedroom across from his office, staring at a large cardboard box strewn across the floor.

"What is it?" she exclaimed.

"It's the *Charlie Russell* paintings my mother gave us from the time my family lived in Wyoming." he replied, gesturing at the large cardboard box on the floor.

"I haven't had time to hang any of them yet." Kay replied, staring at the upended box. "Is that what fell?"

"Oh, it didn't just fall. All the other paintings in the collection are still stacked securely. See?" he said emphatically, deliberately testing the stack of paintings for any indication of movement.

"Heavy stacks of paintings don't just fall. Each package in this stack probably weighs twenty pounds and they have been sitting securely in this room for weeks. That one was pushed deliberately by something intent on getting our attention." he asserted, gesturing at the upended box on the floor.

"What do you think we should do?" she asked, nervously.

"The only thing that sends them away is prayer. I prayed the Holy Scriptures directly to the Father in Heaven when I was surrounded by them at the crash site. They were gone in no time!" he stated, snapping his fingers for emphasis. Their brief discussion on prayer effectiveness against the demonic realm is suddenly interrupted by a second crashing sound downstairs.

"We better check on the dogs!" he exclaimed, exiting the upstairs bedroom with the shotgun at the ready, and heading for the staircase.

"Father in Heaven, hear our prayer, and rid our home of all dark forces that have invaded this place." Kay prayed, following a few steps behind Steve as the two of them carefully made their way downstairs.

Entering the living room, the couple is greeted by two wide eyed, and bewildered German Shepherds, exuding the fact that something wasn't quite right. Neither dog appeared to have been affected physically, however their fearful demeanor was a certain indicator of trouble.

"You're okay. You're okay." he whispered, in as soothing a voice as he could muster under the circumstances. Carefully examining each dog, and the living room environment around him before proceeding, he then moved cautiously toward the kitchen, with the shotgun in hand. Turning on the overhead light, the source of the offending crash immediately becomes apparent, as he stares idly at a large can of dog food in the middle of the kitchen floor. The can had obviously been dislodged from a nearby pantry, and it hit the floor with sufficient force to awaken anyone that hadn't heard the *Charlie Russell* paintings fall upstairs. What had dislodged the can from the overhead kitchen pantry in the middle of the night defied any natural explanation.

"They're just taunting us." Kay decreed, recovering the can and replacing it on the pantry shelf. "There's no way this heavy can moved on its own."

"They're very disruptive when they don't get their way." he insisted. "I was their patsy for a long time and they got used to it. They don't like being outed and having their plans disrupted."

"Do you think we can go back to sleep after all of this?" she asked doubtfully.

"No. My body is still on London time anyway. My stomach is ready for breakfast. I'll wait a few hours and then give that theologian a call. Maybe he'll see me today. I have a trip scheduled for day after tomorrow and I'd really like to see what he says before I leave town again." he declared, pulling a chair out from the kitchen table and carefully setting the shotgun down before taking a seat.

"That's where I was sitting when that Glenn Miller music started playing in your office." she offered, as they eyed one another knowingly.

"And remember … I was still doing their bidding when all that happened. I guess they just couldn't resist taunting and then physically assaulting you."

"I think they've always been committed to our ultimate spiritual and physical destruction. We were both just useful idiots for a time." Kay suggested.

Several hours later, Steve has a meeting scheduled with a senior theologian at a well renowned university seminary in the Atlanta Metro area. Steve is not optimistic, but he is committed to giving the established religious hierarchy one last opportunity to inject meaningful insight and wisdom into this complex, other-worldly struggle. Carefully managing his expectations, he strolls into the senior theologian's office, where he is greeted warmly and directed to a nearby chair. Unlike his previous church hierarchy encounter, the seminary atmosphere is considerably more business-like, with a strong undercurrent of sincerity, dedication, and overall commitment.

"Good afternoon, Mr. Lacey. I'm Dr. Monroe ... but you may call me David." the man insisted, shaking Steve's hand firmly and prompting him to be seated.

"Hello, I'm Steve." he replied, as both men studied each other momentarily. "Thank you for seeing me on such short notice, David."

"No problem. No problem at all. Your pastor, Dr. Williams and I talked a bit about your situation. He was anxious for us to have this conversation. He said he felt like he wasn't able to properly address your concerns during his meeting with you. He's a good man, but a full time pastor runs himself ragged most of the time." the theologian offered.

"I understand ... it's a thankless job." Steve replied, flashing the theologian a disarming smile.

"Now, I believe that you have a spiritual matter of a rather serious nature?" Dr. Monroe prompted. "Please feel free to elaborate on exactly what it is that you have been experiencing."

"Thank you ... My wife and I are in the middle of a high stakes and extremely intense spiritual battle." Steve declared. "We have ..."

"I'm sorry to interrupt you, Steve, but exactly why do you believe that it's a spiritual battle you're fighting?" Dr. Monroe interjected.

"Why?"

"Yes, why exactly do you feel that it's a spiritual battle?"

"Because I've been woefully deceived since my earliest recollections as a child, by an entity masquerading as my deceased uncle. The entity has interacted with me regularly throughout my lifetime and it would manifest physically under certain adrenaline filled circumstances. For several years, I thought that the entity in question was my guardian angel."

"I see … and now you're in some kind of a battle with this entity?"

"Not, just him, but his entire crew and passengers … at least fifteen entities. It started when I refused to participate in their master-plan to spiritually deceive massive numbers of people."

"Deceive them how?"

"By accepting top-secret information that was supposedly permanently inaccessible in a highly classified government file. The entities made the information available to me supernaturally as a demonstration of their power to manipulate and control, in an effort to deceive masses of spiritually vulnerable people." he said emphatically. "They wanted me to share with the entire world how I received the privileged information and then to basically recruit for them. They said that they wanted the masses to know that there was real power available to them in this world if they would just call on it and ultimately worship and serve the dark side. I even heard Satan's disembodied voice when I balked and started asking pertinent questions."

"Oh my …"

"Our spiritual battle became quite heated when I refused to go along with their satanic plan."

"I can imagine!" Dr. Monroe exclaimed, wide eyed.

"They followed me home from England and they have been trying to intimidate me day and night since I returned." he declared, observing the theologian and assessing his reaction.

"You mentioned highly classified information being made available to you supernaturally by these entities? I imagine our government is not too pleased about that? I assume they know you have the information?" the theologian probed cautiously.

"Yes. I've endured their threats and intimidation efforts also. I don't have any allies in this Dr. Monroe, apparently just enemies. The United States Government isn't my primary problem however, they only have a very myopic view of the battlefield. What I need from you is strategic insight into how to win an all out spiritual battle of this sort." he said forcefully. "I've used a Bible repeatedly to ward off all kinds of demonic entities temporarily, but they keep returning. I was wondering if you could suggest a strategy that would handle my spiritual warfare problem on a more permanent basis?"

"I see …"

"The dark side seems undeterred that I've refused to do their bidding and they have resorted to intimidation and fear tactics to try and force me to change my mind." he continued.

"What kind of fear tactics?" Dr. Monroe asked curiously.

"Stalking, manifesting as deceased friends, glaring at me with glowing red eyes, throwing items off shelves, physically assaulting my wife … anything to get inside my head and make me question my faith." he declared, watching the theologian shift uncomfortably in his seat at the graphic and stunning revelation.

"I can see why you feel overwhelmed." Dr. Monroe said sympathetically.

"And outnumbered …" Steve added, gazing at the theologian attentively.

"Well you see, Steve what we do here at the university is train seminary students for church leadership roles. Our resident scholars instruct students on Biblical theory and how that theory correlates to modern church doctrine and various denominational traditions. Basically, we train students to properly administer a church. The battle between good and evil is not really emphasized in our curriculum or for that matter in most modern church doctrine. Those hell, fire, and brimstone sermons make parishioners uncomfortable these days and the modern church has had to adjust to the times." Dr. Monroe stated emphatically.

"Are you saying that you can't help me?" Steve asked point-blank.

"Perhaps I can assist you off the record. Religious institutions, like this one however, must tailor their message and mission to the world around them. Frankly, the world doesn't have any appetite for this spiritual warfare business." the theologian declared.

"I thought the church was supposed to change the world, not the other way around." Steve challenged.

"Well, the church has to adapt and conform to the times or it could go the way of the dinosaur." the theologian answered defensively.

"Church lite?" Steve queried.

"We prefer to call it family oriented."

Pausing for a moment before responding, Steve chooses his next words carefully …

"I understand the dilemma you're facing David, but I should caution you that what you're saying to me sounds an awful lot like the problems with the Seven Churches that Jesus described in the *Book of Revelation* … specifically, the Laodicean Church."

"Well, Jesus also understood the challenges associated with building and maintaining a following." Dr. Monroe countered.

"Yes, but He didn't water down the message of the Gospel to accommodate milk drinkers that never get into the meat of the Word. The Apostle Paul expressly rejected such a notion, and I think we can both agree that spiritual warfare is the meat of the Word."

"I take your point, however church reformation is not why you're here, Mr. Lacey."

"No, it isn't. It's just a shame that with a church on every other block in America, religious institutions still feel that the message of the Gospel must be tailored to accommodate their own weak and beggarly theological delivery system. A problem for another day perhaps … you mentioned off the record …"

"Yes, of course. My suggestion is to use whatever tactic has worked for you in the past. This battle will inevitably come down to a test of wills. Do whatever is necessary to make sure that your will is steadfast and more enduring than the will of the dark forces that are challenging it." Dr. Monroe offered, drumming his fingers on the desk as though awaiting a heavenly epilogue with more detailed insight. The awkward pause continued, morphing into an extended period of silence, with Steve in the unenviable position of feeling like he had just been turned down for a loan at the bank.

"Well, I think I've taken enough of your time, David." he declared, rising to leave and offering the senior theologian a parting handshake.

"Anytime. I hope I have been of some help to you."

"Yes, thank you." Steve lied, trying to appear grateful and deliberately forcing another halfhearted smile.

"I'll share our conversation with Dr. Williams, if that's all right?" the theologian asked politely.

"Surely, and thank you again." he replied, before exiting the theologian's office and nodding politely to the secretary on the way out.

Steve is speechless in the elevator and throughout the long walk back to his truck. Halfway, he spots an empty park bench and decides to stop and phone Kay. Her voice resounds on the third ring.

"Well, did you learn anything that will help us prevail in our battle? she asked excitedly.

"No. It was a complete waste of time. All it did was confirm that, except for our Creator and the Bible, we're on our own. This bunch is so busy playing church, they've forgotten what the real struggle for believers is all about." he said dejectedly.

"Well, come on home … dinner's ready and I'd like you here before it gets dark." she encouraged.

"On my way!"

Chapter Eight

Boomerang

"Put on the full armor of God, so that you can make your stand against the devil's schemes."   *Ephesians 6:11*

The following afternoon, Steve is engrossed in preparations for his upcoming airline trip. After an uneventful night, he dares to entertain the possibility of an informal spiritual cease fire and perhaps a return to some semblance of normal. His musings and trip preparations are mundane distractions, both of which are interrupted by the sound of the front doorbell, and a male voice on the porch declaring …

"Federal Express! Package for Mr. Lacey!"

A chorus of agitated German Shepherds immediately reacts to the intrusion and driver's declaration, barking incessantly as Steve makes his way downstairs. Passing the front door, he exclaims, "just a minute! I need to corral the dogs!" as he moves purposefully down the hallway toward the back door and the fenced yard beyond, with the German Shepherds following closely.

"Good pups! Let's go! Let's go!" he encouraged, opening the door and offering the dogs unfettered access to the back yard, but realizing no interruption to their barking refrain for all his effort.

Moving steadily back down the hallway toward the front door, he peers through the eye level peephole and confirms the presence of a uniformed Federal Express driver before opening the door.

"Sorry about that." he declared. "They aren't good with strangers."

"Yes sir. Please sign here, Mr. Lacey … and again here." the Federal Express driver prompted, confirming Steve's signature before handing him a medium size package with odd handwriting on the shipping label.

"We aren't expecting a delivery. Who is the sender?" he asked, trying to sound casual.

"Let's see … all it says is the village of Black Hameldon, England." the driver replied. "It was shipped three days ago."

"Thank you." Steve said uneasily, surveying the package in considerable detail, assessing its weight and potential contents as the Federal Express driver smiled and turned to leave.

"Have a good day, Mr. Lacey!" he shouted as he climbed back inside his delivery truck.

"Thank you … you too." Steve replied, gingerly holding the package like it might detonate any second.

Back inside the house, he cradled the Federal Express parcel and walked very deliberately toward the kitchen at the rear of the first floor. There, he gently deposited the package on the kitchen table and stared purposefully at it for several seconds.

"What is it?" Kay asked, suddenly appearing in the doorway from the deck area and back yard.

"Where were you? Didn't you hear the dogs barking?" he asked pointedly.

"Everybody in the neighborhood heard them. I've been working in the flower bed in the back yard." she replied. "What is it? Were you expecting a delivery?"

"No. I haven't the slightest idea what it is, only that it was shipped three days ago from Black Hameldon, England." he replied warily, before carefully probing the package with a small kitchen knife.

"That could be good or bad." she conjectured, watching Steve repeatedly perforate the package surgically before finally electing to open it.

"Here goes!" he declared, exhaling deeply before slicing through the last fold and opening the package.

"Isn't that …?" Kay stammered.

"Well, I'll be!" he gasped. "It sure is! It's Ray's Bible! I haven't seen it since I mounted it on that crest overlooking the crash site. I never expected to see it again."

"Are you sure it's Rays?" she asked hesitantly, as he gently grasped the small, well-worn Bible and removed it from the Federal Express package.

"Oh yes, I'm sure." he replied, pointing to the still discernible writing inside the Bible's cover, displaying Ray Wilkins name and Army Air Corps. serial number.

"There's a letter with it." she said, retrieving a folded, handwritten, one page letter from the interior of the package. "It's from a Mr. Ian McShane. Isn't he the man you met at the Damion Pub that night with the horrendous story about being attacked by all the entities at the crash site?"

"Yes, that's him." he replied. "Why on Earth would he be writing me?"

"Well, let's find out …" Kay said, as she began reading McShane's letter aloud. "He says … Dear Steve Lacey, the grateful residents of Black Hameldon, England are returning this Bible to you and your family, with our heartfelt thanks for everything you did on our behalf at the crash site. We wanted you to know that we collected the fifty pounds British Sterling reward from the Scottish tourist and used it to purchase a brand new King James Bible from our local bookstore. The new King James Bible is now securely mounted where we found this one, and there was enough money left over to pay the shipping charge to return your Bible to you. The new Bible that we placed at the crash site seems to be just as effective at spiritually cleansing the area, and we want to say thank you to all the Lacey's by returning this family heirloom to you with our best wishes and gratitude. I'm especially grateful that you ignored my ramblings and poor manners at the Damion Pub that evening and were able to successfully complete your investigation into the Black Hameldon Bomber crash. Everyone in the village wanted me to let you know that there have been no reported encounters with anything supernatural since your visit and we are extremely grateful for your efforts. I understand that this is the second time this Bible has been returned to America, and we hope that now it will be with your family forever. Thank you again for everything. Sincerely, Ian McShane …"

"Well, how about that?" Steve exclaimed, staring at the handwritten letter, as he simultaneously caressed Ray's Bible. "I must say … opening Ian McShane's spiritual eyes is truly a miracle in itself. He was pretty crusty and unbelievably jaded about all of this. I didn't think he had a letter like that in him."

"What on Earth are you going to do with Ray's Bible?" she asked curiously.

"I don't know. I never expected to see it again. Maybe I'll carry it with me in my flight bag with all the other manuals. It's the ultimate operations manual." he quipped, offering her a mischievous grin as he continued to caress the small Bible.

"That was awfully nice of Mr. McShane and the other people in Black Hameldon. We must be sure and send them a thank you note." she prompted.

"Will do. I'll try and …"

"Wait … did you hear that?" she interrupted.

"What?"

"Listen! It's right above us!" she exclaimed.

Both of them stare dumbfounded at the ceiling for several seconds, and then at one another in wide eyed wonder, as the mournful sound of Glenn Miller's *Moonlight Serenade* reverberates overhead. The haunting melody steadily increases in volume, accompanied by what sounds like a large gathering of shuffling feet and accompanying low pitched, unearthly voices.

"My office!" he exclaimed. "They're in my office!"

"That's the same song I heard when you were in England! No question!" she declared.

"Stay here!" he ordered.

Without pausing to assess the risk, Steve cradles his newly reacquired Bible, and makes his way purposefully down the hallway toward the main staircase. Reaching the stairs, he steps cautiously onto the first step, but the music doesn't stop as it had when Kay tested and withdrew. Instead, it grows progressively louder. His office is still not visible from this position, but he is convinced that his private sanctuary has been invaded by a hoard of uninvited demonic guests, engrossed in seditious behavior, amid a backdrop of heartsick Glenn Miller music.

Clutching Ray's Bible for spiritual armor, he proceeds cautiously up the staircase, pausing deliberately on each step to assess the unfolding situation ahead, as Kay recites *Psalm 91* from memory, behind him …

"If you make the Lord your refuge. If you make the Most High your shelter, no evil will conquer you, no plague will come near your dwelling. For he orders his angels to protect you wherever you go. They will hold you with their hands to keep you from striking your foot against a stone …"

Peering around the corner at the mid-point of the angled staircase, he stares in horror as over a dozen shadowy, satanic figures, clustered inside his office, sway rhythmically to the hypnotic music. Their guttural voices are boisterous and demonstrative, but indecipherable. To him, it is evident that their very presence is a fiendish attempt at dominion through intimidation. Undeterred, he continues moving carefully up the staircase toward his office, with Ray's Bible strategically positioned in front of him, like the armor of God. Ahead of him, the eerie, shadowy figures continue to sway rhythmically as Glenn Miller's *Moonlight Serenade* plays repetitively at an ever increasing volume.

Undeterred, he covertly closes the remaining distance, determined to reclaim his home and office from the unwanted, ghostly intrusion. Summoning all his faith and courage, he recklessly charges the remaining interval and forcefully enters his office, fully prepared to do battle to protect his home and loved ones. Instantly, he is confronted by fifteen pairs of seething red eyes, and an overwhelming sensation of crippling nausea that abruptly sends him impotently to his knees.

In milliseconds, he finds himself surrounded by a hoard of vile, abject evil entities, unable to draw his breath as unseen hands close around his throat. His inability to breathe quickly becomes both life threatening and overwhelming, as ghostly hands clasp viciously around his nose and mouth. Fighting for the breath of life is the only thing keeping him from vomiting uncontrollably in response to the crippling nausea. In an instant, his body collapses uncontrollably, face first to the floor, as Ray's Bible drops heavily beside him. He is helpless, surrounded by overpowering evil that is bent on expressing its domination and extreme vexation. Motionless on the floor, he tries to call for help to rebuke the demonic hoard, but his words are choked off by the attackers and drowned out by the blaring music. All he can offer is gasping silence. Mere seconds into the much anticipated demonic counterattack, he has been reduced to a quivering mass of total surrender and helpless resignation.

"Lacey! Lacey!" the demons chant, as ethereal fists begin striking him forcefully from all directions and he reels from the physical onslaught and writhing pain.

Just as the hoard begins violently contorting his extremities, and with his vision narrowing from the deadly lack of oxygen, he bears witness to the sudden, glorious presence of an exquisite, majestic, beam of light. Its source is an absolutely magnificent looking, angelic being, radiating light as bright as the noon-day sun. The being's overpowering presence instantly disrupts the ear piercing *Glenn Miller* music and repels all the demonic intruders that had been entrenched in his office. In addition, anything throughout the Lacey home, opposed to the will of God, is collaterally eliminated.

Within moments, he can breathe again, and the nausea that had caused his knees to buckle, slowly begins to subside. Recovering slowly to his knees, he gazes steadily into the gallant, regal face of a luminescent, other-worldly being, with piercing, yet comforting eyes, that completely inhabit Steve's soul and spirit. Steve is awestruck and utterly captivated by the radiant, angelic being as it hovers nearby and boldly declares, "behold, I am Nathan, a charge of Gabriel. I have been sent to cast out those tormenting you. They are first among the hierarchy of darkness and not subject to your simple rebuke. Gabriel has now forbidden their presence from you and your family. You no longer have anything to fear from them. Stand and be well!" the angel proclaimed as its radiance began to subside ever so slowly, until it eventually disappeared altogether.

"Steve? Steve? Are you all right?" Kay shouted from the staircase.

"Stay there! Give me a minute!" he ordered, trying to gather himself and assess the safety of his immediate surroundings before encouraging her to enter. With his vision slowly returning to normal, his eyes sweep the room anxiously, looking for any sign of the threats that had dominated the environment only moments before. Then, he notices the first clock, and then another, and another, as his relief begins to take hold. Only after checking every timepiece in his office, does he feel confident enough to call out to Kay.

"It's safe now! You can come up!"

Peering cautiously through the doorway, Kay is tentative and hesitant, still weakened from the encounter with the vile energy source that had completely disabled both of them so effectively.

"It should be all right now." he offered with a weak smile. "Look at the clocks! The clocks!"

Still holding the door for support, Kay peers curiously at each clock and individually verifies that they are all operating normally. None of the clocks remain spiritually frozen at 3:24. All of them now reflect the correct time. Retrieving Ray's Bible from the floor, Steve notices that it is miraculously open to *John 3:16,* the same page it was opened to at the crash site in England decades ago. The only evidence of the trauma that just transpired in his office is the slight weakness both of them are still experiencing.

"I've never felt anything so repulsive!" she gasped. "I thought I was going to puke all over the carpet! It must have been even worse in here!"

"Actually … I was more concerned with being strangled to death. Puking isn't an option when you're being strangled." he joked, staggering to his feet and steadying himself awkwardly against the office wall.

"Who was that I heard talking to you?" she asked curiously.

"That was the most beautiful being I have ever seen. He said his name was Nathan, a charge of Gabriel. He stood right there shining like the noon-day sun." Steve declared, gesturing toward the corner of his office.

"Gabriel?"

"That's what he said."

"Gabriel is an archangel, one of the most powerful angels in God's army. Nathan must have been miraculously summoned by either Ray's Bible or by my reciting *Psalm 91.*"

"Well, that makes sense. He said the fifteen demons that were here were first among the hierarchy of darkness and not subject to my simple rebuke. We were basically helpless against them."

"What chance do we have against them if they aren't subject to our rebuke?" she asked nervously.

"He said Gabriel has forbidden them from inhabiting our physical and spiritual space. It's the ultimate restraining order." he joked uneasily, trying to lighten the mood.

"What about Ray's Bible?" she asked curiously.

"It opened to *John 3:16* when I dropped it on the floor. Apparently, it's arrival in the battle is one of the actions that summoned Nathan. Evidently, first among the hierarchy of darkness requires both spiritual armor and direct heavenly intervention to repel them. Now, we have both."

"Are you going to feel like flying your trip tomorrow after all of this?" she asked, eyeing him warily.

"Oh, I think I'll be okay to fly. It's whether or not you feel safe here alone … that's my main concern."

"Well … if Gabriel and Nathan are watching over us, my faith is certainly strong enough to trust that everything will be fine. We were quite limited against the first hierarchy demons anyway, even together in our own home."

"Are you sure you're okay with it?"

"I'll be fine. But, it occurred to me that I really do need to call my Uncle Wohali. I haven't talked to him for several weeks and I'd really like to hear what he has to say about all of this. He's not only a pastor, but a member of the Tribal Council of the Cherokee Nation. He and Aunt Awinita are two of the most spiritually minded believers that I know. They're an hour behind us in Oklahoma, so I still have time to call them this evening."

"Okay … tell them I said hello and that I'm on board with whatever he suggests. A different perspective from people that are that spiritually enlightened is always helpful."

"I remember Uncle Wohali used to emphasize the power of a praying parent whenever he talked about employing the full armor of God. Your parents and grandparents praying for you undoubtedly led to your salvation and kept you safe all those years when you were a bush pilot. What you thought was the result of having Ray Wilkins as a guardian angel was more likely the result of praying parents."

"Well … it certainly hasn't been easy coming to grips with the fact that my supposed guardian angel was actually a demonic impersonator luring me toward eternal destruction. I'd much prefer to think that I survived all those life threatening experiences in an airplane because my parents and grandparents were praying for me."

"If I know Uncle Wohali and Aunt Awinita, our prayer circle will grow quite a bit right after I talk to them. The Cherokee people are very spiritual and this is something they will likely want to share with their entire congregation.

Chapter Nine

Common Ground

"But the meek shall inherit the earth, and shall delight themselves in the abundance of peace."   *Psalm 37:11*

Four uneventful days pass, and Steve is driving home from the Atlanta airport, stuck in heavy traffic, anticipating three scheduled days off before the trip cycle repeats. Kay was almost giddy, anxious to share something important when he called, but opting to wait until he got home rather than share it with him over the phone. All she would say is that it involved Uncle Wohali and the Cherokee Nation in Tahlequah, Oklahoma. Steve's appreciation for the enhanced spirituality of Native-Americans was fostered at an early age by his exposure to life on an Indian reservation. Steve's father, a geologist for a major U.S. oil company, was assigned to a Montana Indian reservation for several months when Steve was very young. With Tribal Council approval, the Lacey's lived in reservation housing, enabling Steve and his family to fully immerse in Native-American culture for a short time.

After successfully navigating Atlanta traffic, he arrives home thirty minutes later, and is greeted by Kay standing at the door, looking almost giddy with anticipation. Thankfully, she doesn't appear distraught or fearful, like she had been after her solo encounter with the Glenn Miller music in his office. Her mood this time is upbeat, with an undercurrent of excitement, obviously stemming from her desire to share good news with him.

"Hi Honey. How was your trip?" she asks coyly, kissing him softly on the cheek, but plainly bursting with anticipation.

"Uneventful … exactly what I needed." he replied, eyeing her expectantly for a moment before asking, "are you going to keep me in suspense?"

"Well … I talked to Uncle Wohali three or four times while you were gone, probably an hour each time. I told him everything that has happened to us since this all started. He promised that he would have his prayer team put us on their prayer list."

"Okay, that's good, but it can't be why you're so excited."

"No. Uncle Wohali and Aunt Awinita have invited us to Tahlequah! They want us to share all our spiritual experiences with the Cherokee people!"

"What?"

"As you know ... Native-American people are very spiritual." she said proudly. "Uncle Wohali wants you and I to share what we've learned with the Cherokee Nation. He wants them to know and understand the spiritual lessons we learned; especially the lesson about discerning dark spirits that masquerade as angels of light."

"How would we do that?"

"Uncle Wohali has already obtained permission from the Cherokee Tribal Council, and if you agree, he wants us to share our experiences publicly."

"Publicly?"

"Publicly among the Cherokee Nation. He wants to reach every member of the tribe ... over 300,000 people around the world. Uncle Wohali believes the auditorium at Northeastern State University would make an excellent forum to share what we've learned with the Cherokee Nation. He said the majority of Cherokee's in Tahlequah are believers, and many Biblical scholars believe that the Cherokee Nation is directly descended from the Hebrew Tribe of Gad. That belief coincides with the Biblical dispersion of the Twelve Tribes of Israel. He feels that because of their Biblical heritage, they must know and understand spiritual matters better than not only the American population, but light years beyond the rest of the world. He said its all related to Native-American relevance in the Biblical end times scenario, as depicted in the Bible's *Book of Revelation*. In the meantime, he doesn't want Native-Americans corrupted by Hollywood, modern American pop culture, or the secular mass media."

"Well, I can appreciate that, but I'm not sure that sharing our experiences publicly is a really great idea. Remember how Eastern Airlines reacted to that story about the apparition of their dead flight engineer from flight 401?"

"Do you really think anyone from the airline industry or the rest of the world is going to care about a speech to the Cherokee Nation on spiritual activity and discernment?" she challenged. "Besides … this is important. We're talking about the spiritual well being of thousands of people, God's people. They are not only especially receptive to hearing our spiritual experiences, but they are destined to play an important role in Biblical end times. We need to share what we've learned about spiritual discernment with them."

"All right, all right, but we may be begging to live in the Cherokee Nation if my employer gets wind of it." he declared reluctantly.

"O ye of little faith." Kay teased, hugging him tightly to seal the deal.

Eight days later, Steve and Kay are backstage at the main auditorium of Northeastern State University in Tahlequah, Oklahoma. The well regarded regional university, located on the grounds of the Cherokee Nation, is the historical site of one of the first female seminaries in the United States. Grounded in the Christian faith , the university serves to advance principles of Christianity and the Cherokee heritage throughout Oklahoma and beyond.

With only minutes remaining before the start of the presentation, the large auditorium is nearly filled to capacity as the steady stream of people entering the room finally begins to thin. Peering out from behind the curtain, Steve is filled with apprehension as he watches the capacity crowd gathering. Glancing around at Kay, he doesn't detect the slightest hint of uneasiness or any misgivings in her. Downplaying his own, he asks Uncle Wohali about the Cherokee people not able to secure a seat in the soon to be filled auditorium.

"Most everyone in the Cherokee Nation has access to a radio and we've been promoting this presentation all week. The extra microphones are for the people that couldn't get here in person." Uncle Wohali replied thoughtfully.

"You mean we're going to be on the radio?" Steve exclaimed, shifting his weight awkwardly.

"Yes, we will be live on every Tahlequah Christian radio station. The presentation is also being taped by secular radio stations for broadcast at 10:30 PM. All the radio stations in Tahlequah will simulcast the presentation in English and Cherokee, for the benefit of our older citizens. Citizens of the Cherokee Nation around the world, not able to hear the broadcast, will read about it in our monthly tribal newsletter. The newsletter is distributed to every Cherokee Nation citizen worldwide, regardless of their residence, and to all our fellow Native-American tribes in Oklahoma."

"Fellow tribes?"

"Yes … Choctaw, Miami, Creek, Iowa, Wichita, Cheyenne, Arapaho, etc. We want to be a messenger of the Great Spirit and share this critical lesson with all of them. It's important that every Native-American understand their role in this spiritual battle and for us to reiterate that they are destined to inherit the Earth once again. Now … to get things started … I'll make a few comments, and then introduce both of you as my guests and relatives. Then, all you have to do is come forward and share your amazing story. Just tell it the way you remember it. Don't worry about the language or cultural differences. Everyone has been told to expect the auditorium presentation by a couple from Atlanta in English."

"Right … and hopefully none of it gets picked up by cable television or satellite." Steve countered, glancing warily at Kay as Uncle Wohali smiled broadly, pulled the curtain back, and walked toward the podium.

Clasping Ray's Bible with one hand and Kay's hand with the other, Steve listens anxiously to the opening portion of Uncle Wohali's address to the Cherokee Nation ...

"The breath of the Great Spirit inhabits every living thing. It is that breath that gives us life. When our spirit leaves the physical body, the body dies and our spirit returns to the Creator. But there are also dark spirits that appear as angels of light. They roam the Earth, looking for those that will submit and surrender to their deceptive temptations. Everything that glitters is not gold, and the dark spirits I am referring to are masters of disguise.

The Great Spirit has infinite wisdom in all matters, while our wisdom is finite. Even as believers, most of us fail to understand eternal realities. Such wisdom is reserved for those that seek, pray, trust, obey, and rely entirely upon the leading and guidance of the Great Spirit. The dark forces seek to diminish the wisdom of the Great Spirit, and many generations have been taught to depend on untrustworthy, alternative spiritual sources. They have negated the true voice of wisdom, and encouraged others to rely on dark spirits for wisdom and guidance. This gives the powers of darkness a stronghold that is not easily broken. It is only when we are faithful and walk according to the wisdom and direction of the Great Spirit that we are able to guard ourselves against such deception.

We all know the fundamental instructions of the Great Spirit, and yet many still reason away that wisdom and lean on their own limited understanding. Disregarding and rejecting the instructions of the Great Spirit, by default, puts you into spiritual agreement with the darkness. That essentially gives the dark spirits permission to enter into and control your lives. It is much easier to let them in than it is to usher them out. We all must make the decision who we will surrender to and serve. It is a decision that is made with every thought and deed.

No two people take the same path or have the same beliefs. That leaves a great deal of leeway for spiritual deception to inhabit and manipulate our earthly reality. Every path and every belief will lead us in one of two directions, either light and truth, or darkness and deception. The Great Spirit is always watching over us, but He will never enslave us. We are given free will to choose which spiritual path we walk. Free will is a precious gift from the Great Spirit and He honors our freedom to choose. Our spiritual enemy therefore only rules over us through our ignorance, weakness, and lack of understanding. Our lack of spiritual insight provides an open door to mental, physical, and spiritual enslavement. The dark spirits will use anything that appears to be acceptable in the eyes of the world, to deceive, manipulate, and control.

The Great Spirit longs for us to choose to willingly enter into fellowship with Him, a decision that results in a loving, trusting, eternal relationship. The forces of darkness stand ready to take advantage of our spiritual miscues and mistakes. Obedience to the Great Spirit however, provides us with a supernatural hedge of protection against the forces of darkness. Ignorance and disobedience to the wisdom and guidance of the Great Spirit removes that supernatural hedge of protection and opens the door for darkness to enter.

The dark side may seem like a harmless, enticing fairy tale, but their ultimate goal is to bring about everyone's complete destruction. A lack of awareness to this reality is why our guests this evening have been at the mercy of such manipulation. They initially rejected the wisdom of the Great Spirit and allowed dark spirits to enter through an open doorway. Thankfully, they have come out of the darkness and into the light of wisdom and truth. Spiritual truth, in conjunction with wisdom and obedience to the Great Spirit, are the only spiritual weapons that mankind has available to defeat the enemies of the souls of men."

As Steve listened attentively to the spiritual commentary, Uncle Wohali transitioned to the Native Cherokee language. Regardless of his inability to understand the Cherokee language, Steve is convinced that in any language, Uncle Wohali is without question a gifted orator, providing sincerity and enthusiasm for spiritual matters that actually required no translation. As a pastor, he had been especially interested in the supernatural aspect of Ray's Bible, and although Steve couldn't understand the Cherokee language, he felt certain that Uncle Wohali was incorporating a brief synopsis of Ray's Bible into his extensive introduction. At the end of the lengthy narrative, he heard his name called, and watched the curtain part in front of him as Kay led him onto the stage.

The large auditorium was filled to overflowing, and the audience looked even more impressive from the podium than it had from behind the curtain. The number of microphones on the stage conveyed the gravity of tonight's topic, and the serious message Uncle Wohali hoped to communicate to his fellow Native-American people. Placing Ray's Bible slowly and deliberately on the podium, Steve let its positive energy flow through him for several moments before beginning to speak …

"I want to thank all of you for coming this evening to hear our story in person. My name is Steve Lacey and this is my wife, Kay. We're here to share our experiences with you and to make you aware of a massive deception being perpetrated on humanity by the spirit world. I'm not referring to deception or deceit by the Lord's angels or anything of a Godly origin. I'm referring to fallen angels, demons, including Satan himself, that successfully masquerade as angels of light. The lesson we are here to share with you this evening, the two of us learned the hard way, and we offer it to you now in Christian love, as a blunt warning, a word to the wise if you will. The admonition we share is actually quite simple, however the God of the Bible requires that it be accepted unilaterally and applied continually, for human beings to avoid becoming casualties of satanic deception during spiritual warfare.

The fundamental lesson that we are here to share with you is that the God of the Bible, the entity that you refer to as the Great Spirit, does neither endorse nor make exceptions to His written Biblical directives. Specifically, the Biblical directive against communicating with the dead needs to be respected without exception. The Word of the Lord specifically states that "*the dead know nothing.*" "What must also be emphasized in conjunction with respecting all of God's written Biblical directives is symptomatic of a much deeper spiritual problem, one grounded in the misguided, satanically inspired culture of the modern world.

Kay and I learned firsthand that to succeed in spiritual warfare against the dark side, you must first understand and accept that you are in a spiritual battle for your eternal soul. Second, you must set aside the culturally accepted norms of the modern world, and avoid any and all spiritual dalliances that are counter to God's written Biblical directives. Black magic, witchcraft, fairy tales, Ouija boards, ghost hunting, angel worship, or any activity that seeks or promotes wisdom or power apart from the Lord is expressly forbidden. There is no such thing as an innocent excursion into the spirit world. Once you open the doorway that leads beyond the veil, everything from that point on has serious consequences.

For me, this spiritual lesson began as one of my earliest childhood recollections. At the age of three, innocence abounds, and there is no awareness that such interaction is either abnormal or potentially dangerous. The innocence of youth makes children especially vulnerable to demonic interference and counterfeit attempts at relationship development. When I was a child, my first encounter with such an attempt involved an entity impersonating my deceased uncle, and it occurred while I was lovingly surrounded by adult relatives, including my mother. Sometimes the encounters were simply hearing a disembodied voice, but many times they involved direct physical interaction with the counterfeit entity appearing as my deceased uncle. Both methods of interaction continued throughout my life, especially during high stakes situations while I was piloting an airplane.

My uncle and his crew had been killed in the crash of a World War II bomber en-route home after the war ended in Europe. The demonic entity impersonating my uncle was supposedly safeguarding me from a similar fate in an airplane. For years, I thought that entity was not only legitimate, but my guardian angel. He even inspired me to assume my current career path as a jet pilot. The real purpose of that fictitious interaction however was to foster a trusting relationship throughout my lifetime, in conjunction with a satanically inspired plan of massive public deception.

The message we came to share with you this evening, is in direct opposition to that satanic master-plan, fostered decades ago and nurtured continually since its inception. The plan involved demonstration of satanic supernatural power, through the revelation of top-secret information that the U.S. Government refused to release regarding my uncle's airplane crash. I received this top-secret information directly from fifteen demonic entities impersonating my uncle's deceased crew and passengers, in a telepathic transference process that essentially made me an eyewitness to the crash. With my supernaturally acquired awareness, the fifty year old mystery surrounding my uncle's crash was instantly solved. When the transference concluded, the entities instructed me to publicly share the source of the satanic, supernatural power and credit them with solving the long held mystery. Their purpose was to entice people to seek the same supernatural power in their lives. Essentially, at the zenith of the satanic master-plan, I was formally tasked with recruiting for the dark side.

But Kay and I came here this evening to talk to you primarily about truth and light. The Bible I am holding, this supernatural book that everyone in my family refers to simply as Ray's Bible, was part of this amazing story before I was born. It belonged to my Uncle Ray Wilkins when he was in service during World War II, and it miraculously survived dozens of combat missions and the crash of his homeward bound bomber. How such a small, fragile item could survive an in-flight explosion, virtually unscathed, was its own stand alone mystery for several decades.

The demonic impersonators of the crewmen and passengers inadvertently showed me how Ray's Bible survived during the telepathic transference process. The Bible fell to Earth from the aircraft's bomb-bay, after the bomb-bay doors separated following the first explosion, and it was found weeks later by an Englishman living near the crash site. The Englishman returned it to our family via the local church that had distributed similar Bibles to every American serviceman from the Shelby, North Carolina area. Although exposed to an explosion and fire, a fall of several thousand feet from a burning airplane, and laying in the open countryside at the mercy of the elements for weeks, you can see that Ray's Bible is in miraculously good condition. The Englishman that found it relayed in his letter that Ray's Bible was open to *John 3:16* when he discovered it. Let me share that passage with you to enhance your appreciation of this amazing book …"

"For God so loved the world that He gave his only begotten Son, that whosoever believe in Him shall not perish, but have everlasting life."

"I first became aware of this very special book when my great-grandmother, Ray's mother, showed it to me as a young child. I already had a developing relationship with Ray's impostor at the time and I could identify Ray in photographs and repeat conversations that I had with his impostor. The fact that he had died years before I was born was a stumbling block for most of the adults in my family. My great- grandmother however was very wise, and she felt that what I really needed was to learn and understand the message of God's Word, and that the teaching vehicle for that should be Ray's Bible. Moved by the supposed connection between her son and I, she directed my grandmother, her daughter, to pass it down to me when I was old enough to truly appreciate its astounding significance.

My uncle's crash, and the mystery surrounding it, were the cornerstone of our family history for decades. Solving that mystery became a burdensome personal quest that blurred my judgment to the point of utter obsession. The military refers to such a level of obsession as "target fixation" and it essentially occurs when a pilot becomes so fixated with dropping a bomb on target that he flies his aircraft directly into the ground. In like manner, I was so obsessed with solving this family mystery that I ignored written Biblical directives, dismissed government warnings, sought assistance from psychics and mediums, and placed my family at ground zero in a spiritual battle against an enemy with dominion over the realm in which we live. That enemy now considers me a traitor and their own arch enemy because I refused to participate in their diabolical scheme of massive public deception.

Rather than participate, what we offer you tonight is a very powerful spiritual antidote, and what we hope to convey is an innate understanding of the hazards associated with participating in this master-plan of deception. Above all else, we hope to impress upon you the danger that the dark side represents to all of us and that they will stop at nothing to deceive, manipulate, and control. The Bible I am holding, Ray's Bible, was ultimately used to spiritually cleanse the crash site in England of demonic activity and to relieve residents of the danger of violent spiritual encounters. Until quite recently, Ray's Bible, was securely positioned at the highest point overlooking the Black Hameldon Bomber crash site in England. It has since been replaced by a brand new Bible, that by all accounts is functionally equally well.

To fully appreciate the significance of this spiritual cleansing, you must understand that upon my arrival in Black Hameldon, England, and before my hike to the crash site, I was informed by locals that no truth existed at the crash site, and that local residents believed it was a portal to hell. My personal experience at the site confirmed many of the allegorical stories of the local residents, and when I ultimately refused to participate in the satanic plan of massive public deception, I heard Satan's disembodied voice expressing his extreme displeasure. He was emphatic that anyone refusing to worship and serve him and his fallen angels would not have any real power in this domain.

It is also worth noting that while I was in England, and prior to my refusal to comply with the master-plan, Kay was at home in Atlanta, being taunted by Glenn Miller music playing on an unplugged stereo in my upstairs office. We later learned from the pilot's widow that the song Kay heard, Glenn Miller's *Moonlight Serenade,* was the last song that the widow and her husband danced to at the Officer's Club the night before he left to go overseas. I'll let Kay share details of that with you momentarily, but you can derive from her experience that it doesn't matter whether you are in total compliance with the dark side or not. They are still committed to deceiving, taunting, and ultimately destroying you.

I know many of you are probably wondering why organized religion wasn't consulted during such an intense spiritual battle? To that I will share that organized religion of the modern world was indeed consulted on two separate occasions for guidance and direction. I am sad and disappointed to report the utter failure of the modern church on both occasions. A spiritual battle requires a measure of spiritual wisdom for any hope of victory, an attribute I found completely missing in the modern church. Instead, I found them more interested in carrying on the traditions of their church and parroting their own man made doctrines. Their total lack of spiritual awareness and insight was not just apparent, but utterly inhibiting to a successful outcome.

On the other hand, spiritual awareness and insight are fundamental attributes of Uncle Wohali. I implore all of you to thank him for his foresight to arrange this presentation and for having the knowledge and wisdom to shepherd all of us in this galactic struggle of good vs evil. He has become our trusted, stand alone spiritual adviser in the earthly realm, but I must share with you a story about direct intervention from the heavenly realm that we experienced recently. It involved a being that identified himself as Nathan, a charge of Gabriel, the archangel. Although I had successfully repelled demonic entities at the crash site and several other locations, by employing Ray's Bible like the armor of God, Kay and I learned that even with Ray's Bible, we required additional assistance during a recent encounter with first tier demonic intruders in our home.

At the height of that dramatic encounter, we were rescued from certain destruction by an angelic being named Nathan, at the bequest of Gabriel. After he rescued us from a tortuous physical attack, he informed us that demonic entities in the first tier of the hierarchy of darkness are not subject to simple rebuke. He also stated that Gabriel had now forbidden all demonic entities, first tier and lower, to intrude on the space of any member of my family, provided we remain obedient to the Word of God. Our lives were spared at the last minute by Nathan's direct heavenly intervention. I would describe him for you as not only extremely powerful, but undoubtedly the most beautiful, majestic being that I have ever witnessed. His sudden, glorious manifestation instantly repelled the first tier demons that had invaded our home and were nauseating Kay and I to incapacitation, while simultaneously choking the life out of us. I would also like to share with you that when I dropped Ray's Bible as a result of my incapacitation, it was a factor in automatically summoning Nathan to our rescue. After our rescue was complete, I retrieved Ray's Bible from the floor of my office and I found it again miraculously open to *John 3:16*. It truly is a supernatural book in so many ways.

While we are discussing heavenly intervention, Uncle Wohali has asked me to specifically mention the power of praying parents and the resulting impact their prayers have on heavenly intervention. It cannot be overemphasized that the power of a praying parent, on behalf of the physical, mental, and spiritual well being of their child, is considered a top priority prayer in the realm of Heaven. I encourage all of you that are parents to stroll boldly into the Throne Room of God and pray without ceasing on behalf of your children.

Before I turn our presentation over to Kay and allow her the opportunity to share her experiences with you this evening, I would like to emphasize two things that are easy to lose sight of in this highly charged, other-worldly discussion. First, it is said that imitation is the sincerest form of flattery, but with respect to my Uncle Ray Wilkins and the James Tyree Bomber Crew, imitation has shown itself to be repugnant, and an incredibly unfortunate disservice. I therefore implore all of you in the Cherokee Nation and elsewhere to include my Uncle Ray Wilkins and the crewmen of the James Tyree Bomber Crew in your formal prayer time. These men stood tall battling Hitler's Nazi Germany during the greatest conflict the world has ever known.

The fact that demonic entities attempted to disabuse and dishonor their sacrifice by using it to their own advantage, does not lessen the magnitude of these men's sacrifice. Even the demonic entities indirectly acknowledged that, when as part of their diabolical masquerade they declared "a sacrifice made out of love of country is a sacred gift."

"The second point I would like very much to emphasize is Native-American correlation to the Biblical end times scenario, and why it is vitally important that all of you remain spiritually pure. Uncle Wohali has asked me to offer these two Biblical references for your edification regarding this very important matter …

"The Tribe of Gad shall be plundered for a time but it will overcome in the end."   *Genesis 49:19*

"In the last days, God declares, "I will pour out My Spirit on all people, your sons and daughters will prophecy, your young men will see visions, your old men will dream dreams."

Acts 2:17

"As part of our commitment to assuring the ongoing spiritual purity of the Cherokee Nation and all Native-American people everywhere, Uncle Wohali has asked us to loan Ray's Bible to the Cherokee Heritage Center for public display to the Cherokee Nation, all Native-Americans, and the visiting public. We have agreed to do so with only one stipulation. All we ask is that while reflecting on the supernatural power of this heaven sent little book and the magnitude of this other-worldly story, that everyone take a moment to honor the James Tyree Bomber Crew from World War II. It is my hope to one day meet the real James Tyree Bomber Crew in Heaven, and until that day, to never be burdened by their imitators again.

And now, I'm going to ask my wife, Kay to share her thoughts and experiences on this subject with you. I believe that once you hear her speak, you will agree that she has a unique perspective on spirituality, as well as extensive experience beyond the veil. Kay if you would please." he beckoned, as Kay arose and approached the podium, hugging him briefly as they exchanged places on stage.

"Hello, my name is Kay Lacey and I'm really excited to have the opportunity to share this with all of you. Before I begin, I would like to thank my Uncle Wohali and Aunt Awinita for arranging this presentation and inviting Steve and I to share our experiences with you. I would also like to offer my personal Native-American lineage for your consideration and hopefully your acceptance. On my mother's side of our family, both my great and great-great grandmothers were full blooded Cherokees. As a matter of fact, my great-great-grandmother was born in New Echo-ta, the original capital of the Cherokee Nation, near present day Calhoun, Georgia. My father's side of our family is equally represented by 100% second generation Choctaw lineage. Both sides of my immediate family reside in Texas and Oklahoma to this day, because over a century and a half ago our ancestors endured the travesty of the *Trail of Tears.*

I have heard and experienced the spirituality of my ancestors since I was a little girl, and because of the Native-American spirituality that we all share, I know that what I am about to tell you will be received without judgment or condemnation. I should preface the details of my first spiritual encounter by saying that experiences of this sort began several years before I was lucky enough to meet Steve. The spectacular nature of what he and I have shared with the Black Hameldon Bomber Crew is certainly unrivaled in its intensity and breadth. But, I believe that my latent Native-American spirituality, in conjunction with a near-death experience that I had as a child, combined to make me especially receptive to matters well beyond our physical world, beginning when I was very young.

The near-death experience I refer to happened when I was a young girl, swimming with friends one Summer afternoon in a rain swollen, Texas canal. After diving into the canal from an elevated platform adjacent to a waterfall, I felt the powerful undercurrent of the waterfall dragging me deeper and deeper down as soon as I entered the water. In mere moments I was struggling helplessly against the undertow, in a futile fight for my life. When those futile efforts ultimately resulted in the large inhalation of water, my spirit actually left my physical body, but remained nearby in the murky canal, as I watched unemotionally while my physical body continued to flail helplessly. I was drowning, moments from certain physical death and unable to save myself.

During the dying process, I felt the presence of Jesus materialize alongside me as I continued watching my body swirling around in crystal clear lucidity, even though visibility in the murky water was almost zero. In the presence of Jesus, I began to experience a complete life review of my time on Earth. At no time throughout the process did I feel anything other than complete peace. It was near the end of my life review that a friend jumped into the rain swollen canal and heroically retrieved my limp body. With the benefit of onshore, life saving first aid, I found myself suddenly back inside my physical body, trying to reorient to the physical world, and respond to those around me.

The memory of that near-death experience has stayed with me to this day, and I have never been afraid of dying since that Summer afternoon in Texas many years ago. One lingering physical side effect has been my inability to maintain a working wristwatch. I have tried repeatedly to wear a wristwatch since that day, but I have never been able to make one run properly for more than an hour. I am told that this side-effect is common among people that have had a near-death event. I believe that the heightened sense of spiritual awareness brought on by such an experience, impacts the flow of energy around the affected person, and it conflicts with mechanisms designed to measure time in the physical world.

I attribute that heightened sense of spiritual awareness to the second experience that I would like to share with you. It is somewhat eerie, but provides a teachable moment for all of us. Not long after my near-death experience, I was asleep in my bedroom, when I was awakened by a strange woman's voice emanating from inside my closet. The closet door, which I had purposefully closed hours earlier, was wide open, and a lovely woman was standing inside the closet. She was well illuminated, and wearing a beautiful gown that was free flowing in a non-existent breeze. The mysterious woman beckoned me to come toward her, calling me by name repeatedly in a very motherly, inviting manner. She also repeated the phrase, "Come here Kay, Hershel wants you" several times, while continually motioning me toward the closet.

Frozen with fear, I did not respond, but remained motionless in my bed all night. The light of morning found me absolutely static in bed and the closet door tightly closed. Electing to head straight for my mother to share the experience, I found my mother uncharacteristically non-responsive to my concerns and ultimately outright dismissive. She insisted that it was all just a nightmare and nothing to be taken seriously. Years later, as an adult, my mother confided in me what she had been unable to share with me that morning when I was a young girl. My mother disclosed that a man named Hershel had been the previous owner of our home and that he had died in the bedroom where I was sleeping.

While I believe that the alluring entity in this experience was decidedly negative, other spiritual encounters I've had have been much less definitive. With respect to the Black Hameldon Bomber Crew, Steve and I suffered galactic confirmation bias, wanting desperately to believe that it was really his uncle and fellow crewmen. The risk of offending a loving spirit that was providing intimate knowledge and acting as a guardian angel totally overwhelmed our ability to discern good from evil, and it spiritually corrupted both of us in the process.

On one particular occasion, while Steve was on a trip and I was home alone, I encountered the other-worldly figure of a man standing in the doorway of our living room. My encounter was brief, but so overt that I felt certain the man wanted more than just my awareness of his presence. He was dressed in World

War II flying attire, and seemed intent on being recognized as one of the Black Hameldon Bomber Crewmen. Shortly after the encounter, I confirmed his identity by reviewing an enlarged photo of the Black Hameldon Bomber Crew hanging in Steve's office. The man's haunting image, pleasant smile, and intense gaze were easily identifiable in the photo since he had been standing in my living room doorway only minutes before. The apparition was totally committed to making me believe that he was the Black Hameldon Bomber's navigator.

I offer that experience to emphasize that a lack of spiritual discernment makes you weak and vulnerable to demonic manipulation and deception. A lack of discernment essentially reduces you to the innocence and vulnerability of a child. The Bible clearly delineates that we are to "*test the spirits*," "not blindly accept their presence at face value to avoid offending them. What we test for is their spiritual alignment with the Word of God. If what is being conveyed, portrayed, or experienced does not entirely align with Holy Scripture, then the source is evil and you must flee from it. The Lord's angels are powerful messengers tasked with carrying communication from the Supreme Being of the universe to human beings awaiting salvation. The Lord's angels serve the Lord unfailingly. They do not stare silently from open doorways, or masquerade as deceased human beings. They do not taunt, manipulate, or deliberately induce fear. They are powerful, swift and sure, not tentative, underhanded and deceitful.

With regard to taunting, Steve mentioned the Glenn Miller music playing in his office in Atlanta only minutes after he encountered an entity mimicking his deceased uncle at the American Military Cemetery in Cambridge, England. I was home alone in Atlanta, something well understood by anyone married to an airline pilot. The fact that the music was emanating from an unoccupied room upstairs, on stereo equipment that was deliberately rendered inactive, was both inexplicable and utterly disturbing. I was not familiar with the title of the song that kept playing repetitively, and it required some trial and error once Steve returned from England, to match the correct song to my memory of the haunting melody.

Eventually, we discovered that *Moonlight Serenade* was the song in question, and within days the pilot's widow of the Black Hameldon Bomber shared with us that *Moonlight Serenade* was played during the last dance she shared with her husband the night before he left to go overseas. They would never dance together again in this lifetime. My point in sharing this encounter is to convey the depth of intimate knowledge that demons retain concerning our friends, loved ones, and ancestors. Fallen angels have been present on Earth throughout human history and they know every human being that ever lived well enough to imitate them. Their knowledge of such intimate details helps them establish credibility with the unwary and non-discerning masses, especially grieving families that are struggling to cope with the loss of a loved one.

I would also like to share with you that over a period of years as an adult, I have been physically attacked multiple times by demonic entities, seeking my complete destruction. Choking and suffocating seem to be the preferred methods of these violent satanic assaults. It's as if the source of their angst with me is the very breath of life itself. As long as I have that breath in me however, I am committed to telling the truth and sharing God's Word with others. For the Bible says *"all believers are ambassadors of Christ and that they must be ready to give an account of their faith, when they are asked to do so."*

"I strongly believe that Native-Americans represent a portion of the "elect" that the Bible refers to in the *Book of Revelation*. It is therefore imperative that Native-Americans of all tribes, remain spiritually pure if they are to be of service to the Great Spirit during the Biblical end times and beyond. A blind guide is of no use to anyone, and the modern, secular world is full of them. I implore all Native-American people to stay righteous and holy. Holy simply means set apart for God's service. To remain holy, you must be able to discern spiritual matters accurately and effectively, and never succumb to the modern, secular philosophy of the empowerment of man. The Bible clearly warns against this misguided philosophy by declaring *"professing themselves to be wise, they became fools."* "Therefore, I encourage everyone listening to this message to follow the Biblical directive which states, *"come out from among them to show yourself worthy to God."* "You can begin by showing reverence to the glorious role in the *Kingdom of God* that the Lord has in store for all of us.

I have learned that historians have documented the presence of Cherokee people in North America since 536 BC. Research has genetically linked members of the Cherokee Nation to the ancient Hebrew tribe of Gad, one of the original Twelve Tribes of Israel. All the ancient Tribes of Israel were dispersed by the hand of God centuries ago in response to gross immorality and flagrant disobedience. They were dispersed, but not forgotten by the God of the Bible. The Bible clearly portrays the role of the Tribe of Gad in the Biblical end times scenario, and its governing role in the future *Kingdom of God*. The *Kingdom of God* is an earthly Kingdom, and the Cherokee Nation, and all Native-Americans, are destined to inherit the Earth once again and to rule and reign with Jesus Christ. The United States of America is not specifically mentioned in the Biblical end times scenario of the *Book of Revelation*. God allowed that entity to punish us for a season because of our flagrant disobedience. In the end however, the return of Native-American people to power and dominion is a Biblical certainty. As you prepare for that reality, I implore you to stay in God's Word, avoid the secular world's counterfeit spirituality, and never forget that you are special in the eyes of the Lord, with your destiny preordained before the foundation of the Earth was laid.

I will now ask my Uncle Wohali to lead us in a Benediction and the sharing of our ancestral prayer, as we give thanks to our Father in Heaven for His forgiveness, and the assurance of our return to His favor and acceptance. May we all be found worthy of such responsibility in God's perfect timing …"

A Prayer of the Great Chief Crazy Horse

"The Red Nation shall rise again and it shall be a blessing for a sick world; a world filled with broken promises, selfishness and separations; a world longing for light again. I see a time of Seven Generations when all the colors of mankind will gather under the Sacred Tree of Life and the whole Earth will become one circle again."

Crazy Horse (1840 - 1877)

Cherokee Prayer Blessing

May the Warm Winds of Heaven

Blow softly upon your house.

May the Great Spirit

Bless all who enter there.

May your Moccasins

Make happy tracks

in many snows,

and may the Rainbow

Always touch your shoulder.

Author Unknown

PART IV

EPILOGUE

Chapter Ten

Full Circle

"I am the Lord your God, who takes hold of your right hand and says to you, do not fear, I will help you."   *Isaiah 41:13*

On the flight back to Atlanta, Steve and Kay are seated together inside the airliner's crowded coach section. Both of them are physically and mentally exhausted from the whirlwind trip to Tahlequah, Oklahoma and the emotional high of sharing their spiritual experiences with the Cherokee Nation. The acceptance and support they received from the Cherokee people was extraordinary, and the outpouring of love and encouragement could not have come at a better time. As the pair settle in for the two and a half hour flight, Kay eyes Steve critically for several moments before suggesting, "you really should try and get some sleep. You look like you're absolutely worn out."

"If I actually look like I feel, I'm probably scaring people." he joked, leaning against the airliner's side window and closing his eyes, anxious to surrender to sleep.

"I'll make sure that nobody disturbs you." Kay offered.

"It's not that … it's the visions I've been dealing with since the transference process. It's all so real, like I was actually there in 1945. The whole gruesome experience lives in my subconscious memory and plays involuntarily again and again in my head. I'm worried that the Black Hameldon Bomber crash will always haunt my sleep."

"Somehow, you have to let it go enough to get some rest. I'll wake you if it looks like you're having another bad dream." Kay suggested.

"Promise?"

"I guarantee it!" she said reassuringly.

"Okay, I don't want the cabin crew to see me having fits, convulsing, or reacting to any kind of stimuli. It could get back to the company. The less they know about all of this other-worldly phenomenon, the better." he insisted. "I don't want to have to explain to my employer or the FAA what's going on in my head."

"I understand dear, get some sleep. Sweet dreams."

"Sweet dreams? Very funny."

"Sorry. It just slipped out." she assured him, watching as Steve leaned against the side window and slowly drifted off into much needed sleep.

June 12, 1945, 09:30 Hrs., Base Air Depot 2, U.S. Army Air Corps., Lancashire, England.

As he walked down the long row of airplanes, Curt Lemond was fidgeting nervously and struggling to keep the explosives concealed under his baggy coveralls. He was very distraught as he shuffled along, searching for his target in the bright morning sunlight. He had never held a bomb before, much less two at the same time, and he was nearly paralyzed with fear as he dragged himself down the long line of heavy bombers. There were dozens of them parked in front of the Air Transport Command hangar, so many that the line stretched across the Air Transport Command ramp and beyond. To him, it looked like the entire U.S. Eighth Air Force was parked at BAD-2 this morning.

Squinting in the bright morning sunlight, he cursed his carelessness for leaving his glasses behind in the truck. The error meant he had to strain to read each bomber's tail-number and his search was taking longer than planned because of it. He'd encountered every possible combination of numbers already, but so far no 5095. The ground crew had no doubt moved her late last night after he and the other O.S.S. men left the work detail.

Shuffling down the long line of aircraft, with the bulky explosives hidden awkwardly under his clothing, Lemond eventually came upon the B-24 he was seeking. For a moment, he stood only yards away from aircraft 5095, pausing to read the tail-number emblazoned on its right vertical stabilizer. Grunting in disgust, he muttered, "66235" and resumed walking, never looking back. If he had, he might have noticed the numbers 5095 on the bomber's left vertical stabilizer as he passed.

Continuing his fruitless search, he strained to read each tail-number, still pursuing his quarry and completely unaware of his galactic error. The fact that aircraft 5095 had undergone a hurried replacement of its right vertical stabilizer at the BAD-2 facility had been of little interest to Lemond or the other O.S.S. men. They were therefore completely unaware that because of time constraints, the tail-number on the bomber's right vertical stabilizer had not been changed when the unit was replaced. Lemond and his O.S.S. associates had always approached aircraft 5095 from the left side when they were manipulating the bomber's engine components and hydraulic lines, and performing other acts of minor sabotage to induce mechanical delays. The fact that there were actually two tail-numbers on aircraft 5095 had gone entirely unnoticed.

As he continued walking down the long column of B-24 heavy bombers, he eventually reached the end without finding his target and became highly agitated. He was afraid James Tyree and the others might have left already for the States. With that in mind, he was heartened when he noticed a lone bomber parked next to the main hangar, some distance away from the others. It was a good thirty yards from him, but he felt certain that it had to be the Tyree airplane. "That must be it!" he exclaimed, approaching cautiously as he struggled to read the distant tail-number. "5095 ... 5095." he kept repeating over and over again as he squinted in the bright morning sunlight.

Unable to completely focus his eyes, he scanned the ramp nervously, relieved to see other ground crewmen working nearby as he continued to approach the lone bomber. Inching closer and closer, he strained to read the distant markings.

"Damn!" he cursed himself again for his absent-mindedness with the glasses. His astigmatism and the bright morning sunlight were both working against him as he kept inching closer, trying to decipher the blurry tail-number. "All right! That's more like it!" he suddenly exclaimed, walking very deliberately toward the open bomb-bay doors of aircraft 42-95695, and about to make a monumentally fatal blunder.

When he reached the bomber's open bomb-bay, he gave the flight crew standing nearby a perfunctory greeting and entered the bomb-bay unchecked. Unknown to Lemond, Aircraft 42-95695 was positioned near the hangar only because the facility's lone fuel truck was out of order this morning. All aircraft requiring fuel at BAD-2 were scheduled to be towed to the fuel pumps next to the main hangar. Aircraft 42-95695 was just the first one of several scheduled to be towed to the hangar in sequence.

Peering inside the bomb-bay, he was tense, expecting to be challenged by her flight crew any minute. Instead of challenging him however, the flight crew appeared indifferent to what he was doing, as they chatted cheerfully under the bomber's right wing. Ed Hickey had instructed him to place both timed explosives inside the open bomb-bay near the center fuel tank, and he immediately began surveying the bomb-bay for a suitable hiding place. As he did, he gingerly removed the explosives from under his coveralls and tried to remain balanced on the bay's narrow catwalk. He would still have to set the timer on each device. Nate Watson hadn't wanted to do it in advance as a safety precaution, or so he'd said. The crudely constructed O.S.S explosive devices had been designed so that the timers had to be set before the arming switches were activated, or so Lemond erroneously believed. He had been so nervous when Nate Watson went over the details with him that he found himself struggling now to remember what he'd actually been told.

With his hands shaking badly, he clutched the first explosive, trying to recall the sequence Nate Watson had drilled into him for arming it. The timers had actually been set to a zero second delay to save the batteries and allow Lemond the chance to calculate a more accurate time delay between arming the device and ninety minutes into the proposed flight. It was done for timing accuracy and preservation of the ignition source, not for safety. He would now have to set both timers, conceal each device separately, and exit the bomb-bay without arousing suspicion.

Fidgeting nervously, he tried to calculate the setting for the first timer by estimating the time the bomber would be ready to depart. With sweat pouring into his eyes, he glanced around the bay uneasily when he thought he heard others approaching outside. His worst fear was being caught with the explosives by the flight crew if they should suddenly appear. They would no doubt beat him severely before finally turning him over to the military police. The notion of being beaten brutally by a dozen enraged men terrified him more than what the bomb might do if he made a mistake. That primal fear was very much on his mind as he eyed the bomb's timer with only a portion of his attention. His concentration was divided between setting the timing device accurately, balancing on the narrow catwalk and wondering what to do if the flight crew suddenly appeared. Pausing awkwardly, he stared blankly at the first miniature clock-like device and listened intently for any sign of the flight crew.

Holding the first timed explosive in his right hand, he wiped the sweat from his left eye with his other hand and enjoyed a momentary reprieve from the stinging, burning sensation. With his right eye filling with sweat also and the irritation becoming unbearable, he decided to switch the explosive to his shaking left hand for just a moment to wipe the sweat from his right eye. In doing so, he enjoyed a temporary reprieve from the intense burning sensation, until the instant his shaking left forefinger inadvertently bumped the bomb's master arming switch. The miscue momentarily displaced the tiny spring loaded arming switch slightly out of the off position. With the bomb's timer still preset to a zero second delay, an enormous explosive blast suddenly shattered the early morning silence of the BAD-2 airfield, as flames and debris shot into the air, and several secondary explosions erupted in rapid succession.

Across the main ramp preflighting his B-17, A.J. Williams felt each concussion and saw the smoke and flames rising high over the Air Transport Command hangar. He didn't know where his good friend, James Tyree was at the moment, and his first thought was for his friend, as he watched thick black smoke billowing over several parked B-24's.

"What the hell happened?" he shouted at the radio-operator.

"A B-24 exploded!" the radio-operator replied, as he listened intently to his headset. The rest of the crew immediately raced to the bomber's viewing ports to look, and stared in awe at the rising smoke column in the distance.

"Who was it?" Williams demanded. "Which crew was it, dammit?" he shouted frantically as the radio-operator listened to an incoming report.

"Uh, Tyree, James Tyree they think, but they aren't sure." the radio-operator replied, as Williams continued staring in horror at the rising black smoke.

"Was anyone in it? Was anyone inside?" Williams demanded.

"They don't know. There are a lot of men missing …" the radio-operator reported, as Williams cringed in response.

From his hilltop two miles away, Ed Hickey exclaimed, "my God!" as he watched the smoke rising high into the air and felt several shock waves rumble across the countryside. "Holy Jesus!" he groaned.

"Do you think Curt got out before it blew?" Nate Watson shouted at him frantically.

"Your guess is as good as mine." Hickey snarled, scanning the distant scene with his binoculars.

"We better get out of here right now!" Watson exclaimed, scrambling to gather their camping gear.

"Not until we know what's happened!" Hickey barked.

"But …"

"We aren't leaving here until we know for sure! No buts about it!" Hickey ordered, drawing his .38 caliber revolver and aiming it directly at Watson's head. "Drop that equipment!"

Instantly frozen with fear, Watson could barely manage, "uh, okay, Ed, okay, whatever you say." as he dropped the camping equipment. "But what now?" What do we do now, Ed?" he implored, as he tried to regain an element of self control and not antagonize Hickey further.

"Now, we check with our contact in operations." Hickey replied coolly, still aiming the revolver at his head. "If it worked, we'd better get those telegrams going right away. They were supposed to be dead two weeks ago, remember?" he snarled, staring into Watson's frantic eyes and back at the rising smoke column.

"Okay, Ed. Whatever you say. I'll check with our contact and see what he knows." Watson stammered, shaking badly as he re-stowed the camping equipment and tried to resume his duties. It wasn't easy with Hickey's .38 caliber revolver aimed squarely at his head.

"Nobody is leaving here until we know for sure." Hickey warned again, slowly un-cocking the weapon and returning it to his holster.

Two and a half hours later …

"I talked to our man in operations again, Ed. You aren't going to like it …" Watson warned.

"What's that supposed to mean?" Hickey growled.

"Well, for someone that was so sure a couple hours ago, he's certainly lost for words now." Watson maintained.

"What do you mean lost for words?" Hickey snapped again.

"Well, now he says aircraft 5095 has been accounted for and so has James Tyree."

"Good God!" Hickey gasped. "Who … who was killed then?"

"Beats me. He said they have twelve men missing right now, not counting ours … a whole crew and some passengers. Paul saw Curt go into the bomb-bay of the airplane that exploded about three and a half minutes before the blast." Watson relayed.

"God Almighty!" Hickey screamed again, pounding his fist against the side of the truck. "What … what do they know?" he demanded.

"Just that there was an explosion and fire. Right now they think it was a refueling accident." Watson replied.

"Jesus!" Hickey snarled, still trying to collect himself. "What about the telegrams?"

"They went out to all the families at 11:50 this morning when everyone was certain it was James Tyree and the others." Watson said somberly.

"God Almighty!" Hickey screamed again, slamming his fist repeatedly into the side of the truck. "Now, we've had them declared dead twice and they're still up and walking around. "God Almighty!" he screamed over and over again, on the brink of losing all control.

"Take it easy, Ed. You've got to get hold of yourself." Watson urged.

"Yeah, sure! I'll get hold of myself! God Almighty!" Hickey exclaimed again frantically, pounding his fist against the side of the truck until it was covered with blood.

Thirty awkward minutes later, when he finally managed to regain a portion of his self control, Hickey approached Nate Watson again and declared menacingly, "It's up to us now, Nate … us. There's still time left if we use it right. There's no turning back now anyway. We've got to see this thing through."

"Okay, Ed, whatever you say. But do you think we can still get close enough after what's happened?" Watson asked curiously, leery of Hickey's .38 caliber revolver and trying not to provoke him again.

"What choice do we have? We've already had them declared dead twice. If they show up back home now people are going to start asking questions and the answers lead right back to us." Hickey fumed. "We've got to do it right this time and there can be no trace of them left! We need them all lost at sea!"

June 13, 1945, 13:20 Hrs., Weather Briefing Office, Base Air Depot 2, U.S. Army Air Corps., Lancashire, England.

"Good morning, Lieutenant."

"Good morning, sir." James Tyree replied, shaking hands firmly.

"You must be feeling pretty lucky after yesterday." the weather briefing officer said with a smile.

"Sir?" Tyree replied.

"A lot of people thought that was your crew yesterday in that refueling explosion." he said candidly.

"Really? No one said anything. I knew it was lucky we weren't being refueled, but I didn't know anyone thought it was us." Tyree said in surprise.

"Well, after that explosion we were only able to get a handful of flights off yesterday, some B-17's." the weather briefing officer said soberly.

"B-17's? That explains it! A friend of mine was supposed to fly a B-17 out of here yesterday and I haven't seen him since. Do you know if A.J. Williams left in that group of B-17's?" Tyree asked curiously.

"Hang on a minute … Williams … Williams … Williams. Yeah, here it is. He left about forty minutes after the explosion." the weather briefing officer stated.

"Oh, Jeez."

"Is there a problem?"

"Well, we were going to try and go together. I hope he doesn't think that was me yesterday in that explosion. He may try and contact my wife!" Tyree exclaimed.

"Oh, I'm sure by now that part of it has been straightened out. They still haven't positively identified the men killed though. Shall we get started?" he urged as Cole Johnson and Stephen Coronado entered the weather briefing room.

13:30 Hrs.

"So, you can see this weak cold front lying along your route of flight between BAD-2 and the Northwestern coast of Scotland is the primary weather maker. You can expect instrument flying conditions for about the first hour or two of your flight and then things should improve considerably. You'll probably encounter light icing in the clouds above 4,000 feet for the first two hours or so, and then it should dissipate." the weather officer continued.

"Uh-huh. What about pilot reports? Has anyone reported more than light icing or moderate turbulence?" Tyree asked.

"No. The only report I had was from a B-17 about an hour ago and it just said light chop all the way until Northwest of R.A.F. Stornoway."

"What about the winds?" Coronado interjected.

"According to the forecast for your route, there will be moderate headwinds most of the way, but your fuel supply should more than compensate for them." he replied. "It's all laid out in your weather packet, everything, including a time and distance calculation to each checkpoint."

"What kind of weather is Meeks Field reporting?" Tyree asked curiously.

"Not too bad, broken clouds, but some fairly strong winds. The last report showed that they were right down the runway though." the weather briefing officer replied as the session continued.

13:47 Hrs.

"Well, that should just about do it then. Are there any questions?" he asked as Tyree, Johnson, and Coronado shook their heads no. "Remember what I said about that instrument approach to Meeks Field. It's the most important thing in all of this." he repeated, shaking hands firmly with each one of them. "Good luck, gentlemen! Have a great trip home!" he said enthusiastically.

"Thank you, sir. This is the one we've been waiting for!" Tyree said with a big grin.

"I can imagine. Best of luck to all of you!" he replied.
Following them to the door, the weather briefing officer anchored himself in the doorway and waved goodbye as they exited the briefing room and walked across the ramp. With their ride home waiting in the distance, he thought for a moment how lucky they all were. They had just won a World War and were going home as heroes. How he envied them!"

"I can't believe we're finally going home after all this!" Tyree exclaimed, as they walked briskly across the Air Transport Command ramp toward their waiting bomber. "I can't wait to see Jennie!"

"I can't wait to see any American girl!" Cole Johnson joked.

"Amen!" Coronado echoed as they ambled along together.

When the three officers cleared the long stretch of concrete and reached the waiting bomber, they found their six passengers waiting outside as Eldon Wilson and the rest of the Tyree crew ran through their preflight checks inside. "Good afternoon, everybody!" Tyree offered, shaking hands all around.

"Good afternoon, sir. Home sweet home, finally, huh?" passenger John Hansen prompted.

"Yeah, finally." Tyree echoed.

"How long is the ride this afternoon, sir?" Hansen asked curiously.

"Oh, about six hours."

"Iceland?"

"You guessed it. Meeks Field, Iceland. I hope everyone has their cold weather gear ready." he prompted.

"Yes, sir, all set!" each passenger replied in turn.

"Okay, then, let's get the party started!" Tyree urged, walking over to the bomb-bay and tossing his bags inside as he climbed up on the narrow catwalk and inside the heavy bomber.

13:54 Hrs.

"Okay, let's have the before start checklist! I won't get to say that many more times!" Tyree mused aloud, a bit despondent that the final leg of their journey would be the last time he and his crew would ever fly a B-24 together. They had all shared the horrors of war and survived when so many others around them had not, an experience that formed a bond that time would never take away. As badly as he wanted to be in Jennie's arms right now, he knew he would miss these men when it was all finally over. The camaraderie and sense of purpose they had shared was something he knew he would always cherish in the years ahead.

14:14 Hrs.

"'Army 5095, you're cleared for takeoff! Have a great trip home!" the BAD-2 control tower announced, as radio-operator Jacob Stewart acknowledged the clearance and quickly relayed it to Tyree.

"Got it, Jimmy. Standby for full power!" Tyree ordered.

He then lined the bomber up with the runway, eased the throttles forward and released the brakes, feeling the acceleration push him back in his seat. Gaining airspeed slowly, the big bomber thundered down the long runway for several thousand feet until it eventually staggered into the air and began a slow climb. When their airspeed margin was adequate, Tyree rolled 5095 into a turn toward the Northwest, and the nearby Scottish border as the bomber immediately entered the low lying stratus clouds.

Watching them disappear into the solid overcast from his adjacent hilltop, Ed Hickey scanned his watch and began anticipating the effect of the first timed explosive charge inside the right wheel well. It would all happen in less than an hour. They were late, but everything was still going according to plan.

"Climb power!" Tyree ordered, as they entered the clouds. "Not much to look at!" he remarked, scanning the flight instruments in front of him as he rolled out on course. "Jacob, advise Air Transport Command we're airborne and climbing to 6500 feet." he ordered as he made several corrections in heading and pitch.

"Will do." Stewart replied, adjusting the frequency on his radio transmitter.

"Pilot to crew … keep an eye out for ice!" Tyree reminded as they continued climbing.

"Navigator to pilot, your initial course is 329 degrees. The heading for wind is 318 degrees. I'll call your turn to the North in 113 miles." Coronado reported.

"Okay, heading 318, thanks, Stephen." Tyree replied.

14:28 Hrs.

"How's it going back here?" Eldon Wilson asked, as he squeezed into the crowded waist compartment and peered outside through one of the bomber's viewing ports.

"Is something wrong?" one of the passengers asked right away, eyeing him curiously.

"No, just checking for ice. There's a cold front pushing through here and we might have to use the boots to clear the ice. Lieutenant Tyree wanted a report, that's all." Wilson said matter-of-factly.

"Oh." the man grunted, resuming his reclined position against the bulkhead and pulling a sleeping bag up over his head.

"Anything you guys need?" Wilson asked, as he surveyed the right wing through the opposite viewing portal.

"No, thanks, we're doing okay." a second passenger replied over the engine noise, as 5095 swayed in the turbulence.

"Okay, just let me know …" Wilson prompted.

14:45 Hrs.

"Navigator to pilot, your course is now 360 degrees." Coronado announced, as Tyree immediately began turning in that direction. "The wind correction angle is 15 degrees left. Make your heading 345 degrees for wind." Coronado stated, as Tyree immediately steadied the bomber on the new heading.

"It's just a trace of ice right now, sir. I'd cycle the boots every ten minutes, though." Eldon Wilson suggested, as he entered the cockpit.

"Okay, ten it is!" Tyree replied, nodding at Cole Johnson, who immediately turned on the anti-icing switches and adjusted the timer.

"Radio to pilot, sir, I'm having a problem with the radio equipment back here. My receiver seems to be losing power steadily and I'm having trouble hearing anybody, even R.A.F. bases a few miles ahead." Jacob Stewart interjected.

"What do you think is causing it, Jacob?" Tyree asked, well aware that the radio would be essential over the open ocean.

"I can't tell. It seems like it's just getting steadily weaker, Lieutenant." Stewart answered.

"Okay, hang on. I'm sending Eldon back." Tyree replied, turning and nodding to Eldon Wilson, who began moving aft.

"Look at the range indicators!" Johnson exclaimed moments later, gesturing at the wildly oscillating needles. "What the hell do you make of that?"

"It must be an electrical problem, probably the same one that's fouling up the radio." Tyree reasoned, pausing a moment before keying his throat mike. "Pilot to engineer, have you found anything back there, Eldon?" he asked.

"Ah, no sir. The radio seems to be getting power. The problem must be in the wiring itself." Wilson replied.

"Well, we're having a problem with the radio direction finders now too. Is there a chance everything's on the same electrical circuit?" he asked hopefully.

"Which D.F. is it, sir?" Wilson replied.

"Both of them. They're dancing all over the place."

"It can't be a power source problem then. They're on separate power sources." Wilson replied.

"Well, when you get finished back there, we could sure use your help up here." Tyree urged.

"On my way!" Wilson exclaimed, eyeing Jacob Stewart again and suggesting, "try checking the tubes. It's worth a shot. I'll be back in a minute." as he turned to exit the radio compartment.

14:50 Hrs.

"Stephen, can you keep up with things over the water without the D.F. as a backup?" Tyree asked candidly.

"Sure, if we keep the turns to a minimum and the wind forecast was accurate." Coronado replied without hesitation.

"Okay, we're steady on 345 degrees." Tyree stated. "Pilot to radio, how's your equipment looking now, Jacob?"

"Oh, it's still getting worse, sir. The signal is so faint I can barely make out anything at all. I can't tell if it's just the receiver or the transmitter, too." Stewart replied.

"Have we passed an R.A.F. base recently, navigator?" Tyree asked point-blank.

"I don't think so, James, but it's hard to tell without the D.F." Coronado replied.

"Okay, listen, I'm going to circle for awhile until we get this thing figured out. I don't want to commit ourselves to the open ocean until we know what kind of a navigation and communication situation we're dealing with. Let's try to get a handle on these anomalies before we go any further." Tyree ordered as he rolled 5095 into a tight left turn. "We should be okay with other traffic at this altitude."

"Yeah, no problem." Johnson replied, nodding in agreement.

"Hell of a situation. No radio navigation and no communication. Lost and silent is no way to fly across the Atlantic ocean." Tyree groaned.

14:57 Hrs.

"We can't keep this up forever!" Tyree barked, keying his throat mike again. "Engineer, what have you got?" he demanded as they orbited above the English countryside inside heavy clouds. From well behind him in the bomber's radio room, Flight Engineer Eldon Wilson replied, "well, Lieutenant, it looks like somebody fooled around with the wiring back here or didn't rack things properly. Either way, most of it is shorted out pretty bad."

"Any chance of getting the D.F. back?" Tyree asked immediately.

"No, sir, I can probably keep it from getting worse, but the D.F. wires shorted out before I got here." Wilson replied.

"What about communications?" Tyree asked hopefully.

"The same. The only lines not affected seem to be the intercom." Wilson declared.

"Okay, get back up here. It looks like we'll have to turn back. I'm not flying to Iceland, deaf and blind! Dammit!" Tyree exclaimed, as he shallowed his bank angle and returned the bomber to straight and level flight. He was just about to ask Navigator Stephen Coronado for a return heading to the BAD-2 airfield when the big bomber was suddenly jolted by a savage explosion on the right side and the simultaneous ringing of the fire warning bell on engine number three.

"Silence the bell! Shut off fuel to engine number three! Feather the prop!" Tyree ordered, pressuring the rudder against the yaw.

"Holy Jesus!" Wilson exclaimed over the intercom, peering outside at the right wing. "Lieutenant, we have major damage to engine number three and the whole leading edge of the right wing!" he shouted.

"Roger! Standby!" Tyree shouted, struggling to bring the damaged machine under control.

"Fire warning on engine number three!" Johnson shouted, as the fire warning light glowed steady red.

"Fire the extinguisher!" Tyree ordered as engine number four suddenly began vibrating also and he pulled its throttle to idle. "Tell whoever can hear us we're declaring an emergency and letting down out of the clouds! Combat stations everybody! Report all ground contacts!" Tyree ordered, as the gunners moved swiftly to man the Liberator's firing stations and search below them for visual clues.

Easing the stricken machine into a shallow descent, Tyree shouted, "Stephen, can you tell if we're over land or water?" well aware that ditching in the sea was suddenly a real possibility if they had been blown off course while circling and no airfield suddenly became available.

"I can't say for certain, James. We've got to be somewhere near the border with Scotland. Hard to say after circling. If we are off course, the high terrain along the coast should still be South of our position. I estimate the R.A.F. Base at Stornoway to be within twenty minutes of us to the Northwest!" Coronado responded.

"Okay, I'm going to spiral down slowly in case we need to stay away from that high terrain along the coastline. Pilot to crew, report all ground contacts and standby for possible ditching instructions!" he ordered, watching the altimeter wind down through 4,000 feet.

"Fire warning still illuminated on engine number three!" Cole Johnson exclaimed.

"Engineer to pilot …" Wilson interrupted. "The fire in the number three engine area is out of control and spreading to the right wing!"

"Roger!" Tyree shouted. "Pilot to crew, we have an uncontrollable fire on the right side. Evacuate the aircraft as soon as we're down! Eldon! Get those life rafts ready just in case!" he ordered.

"Holy Jesus!" Cole Johnson exclaimed as he stared at the raging inferno spreading across the right wing. "What about the chutes? The chutes?" he asked desperately. Pausing before answering, James Tyree thought for a moment how surreal everything had suddenly become. "This can't be happening! We're heading home!" he shouted as he strained to control the crippled machine.

"No chutes! We could be over water! We'd never survive a parachute jump into the water!" he declared, easing the nose down further, desperately searching for ground contact.

15:02 Hrs.

"Navigator to pilot, I can't pin it down that close without the D.F. The coastal high terrain should definitely be South of us, but not by much. Suggest you widen the turn radius to the North to make sure we clear all the high terrain in the descent!" Coronado exclaimed.

"Roger! We'll let down slowly until we break out of the clouds and then if we've been blown offshore, we'll turn back toward the coast if we have to!" Tyree shouted. "If we have to ditch, I want us as close to the shore as possible! Get me a heading for the nearest suitable airfield when you can!"

"Roger!" Coronado exclaimed, as he watched roaring flames inundate the right wing.

Back in the stricken bomber's tail-turret, Eric Irving was absolutely speechless, staring at the thick black smoke trailing off into oblivion behind the aircraft. He knew that the heat source for that smoke had to be tremendous. The perception he'd carried for so many months now about never seeing home again was reaching a climax as he watched the huge black cloud continue to intensify. As he waited at his combat station, he searched desperately through the clouds for visual contact with the ground but to no avail.

15:06 Hrs.

With the altimeter winding down through 1500 feet and the crippled bomber still descending inside heavy clouds, a second powerful concussion suddenly rocked the doomed aircraft. "Son of a bitch!" Tyree shouted as the blast nearly knocked him out of his seat and he fought to stay at the controls of the rapidly disintegrating machine. Behind him, intense scorching heat filled the bomb-bay, as it erupted in flames, and he heard his men screaming in agony.

Groping for the rudder pedals, he found them frozen in position as he tried frantically to free them. In one terrifying instant, he realized that the bomber actually had no rudders left for the pedals he was pushing to control. Before he could express his insight to Cole Johnson, the doomed airplane began pitching up and down violently, shuddering incessantly in its final spasms of life. "Holy Jesus!" Johnson gasped, hanging on as tightly as he could inside the wildly gyrating machine.

"Everybody, stand by for crash landing!" Tyree shouted, manhandling the controls and feeling no effect for his efforts.

Inside the tail-turret, Eric Irving watched huge pieces of both vertical stabilizers separate from the airplane, eliminating all doubt in his mind that he was going to die. Staring helplessly as the pieces drifted off behind him, he felt the ride inside the crippled bomber immediately become an uncontrolled death spiral as he and the others inside braced for the inevitable crash.

15:14 Hrs.

With massive portions of the aircraft now separating from the air frame, and the bomber auguring completely out of control, men screamed for help from the on-board fire raging in the bomb-bay. An intense, fiery, inferno engulfed the right wing and the bomb-bay, as thick, toxic smoke spread throughout the ship and filled the cockpit. Still inside heavy clouds, Tyree sought the ground with all his being as fire tore through them and his men screamed for life itself.

"Power! Power! Power!" Cole Johnson shouted as the descent rate started to steepen out of control. "That's it! Stay with it! Stay with it!" Johnson encouraged, as the bomber continued oscillating up and down, and thick, toxic smoke continued filling the cockpit. "James! James!" Johnson shouted as they broke out of the clouds and to their horror suddenly found themselves face to face with rising, rugged terrain. "Power! Power! Power!" he shouted again frantically, fire-walling the remaining engines, as the nose of the bomber pitched up momentarily.

15:17 Hrs.

The reprieve from the maddening plunge was short lived. Inside 5095, death screams filled the air as intense fire seared through the men, and the badly disintegrating bomber augured wildly out of control. With the ground rushing up to meet it and it's flight controls mangled or missing, 5095 was hemorrhaging to death in an uncontrollable, sweeping descent. Tyree and

Johnson were fighting with all their combined strength to shallow the descent, knowing they were about to impact the rugged terrain, even as toxic smoke filled their lungs and blinded them.

"James! Jesus, James!" Johnson shouted as both of them pulled savagely on the controls. Aside from the suddenness of it, the whole thing still seemed illusory to Tyree, like a nightmare he would wake up from any minute and be grateful it was over as had been the case so many times before. But this was no nightmare. He had actually believed he would keep his promise to Jennie and return to spend the rest of his life with her. He had been betrayed now and was going to die instead. He would never see Jennie's face again. Dear God! He'd broken his promise to Jennie!

Behind him at the radio-operator station, in his last moments of life, Jacob Stewart squeezed his lucky penny tightly and transmitted a final frantic distress call over the emergency frequency. His words were an impassioned plea for help that thanks to the Office of Strategic Services would never be heard by anyone.

15:23 Hrs.

Below in the village of Black Hameldon, England, several people watched in astonishment as the aircraft, whose engines they had heard orbiting overhead for some time, suddenly materialized out of the clouds on fire. The huge bomber was in a dramatic, fiery plunge to earth, in the final throws of absolute peril, seconds from impact, as they all watched in horror.

15:24 Hrs.

With Tyree and Johnson tugging frantically at the controls, trying to shallow the maddening descent, their last hope of surviving the now imminent crash, 5095 suddenly rebelled again. The raging inferno encircling the right wing had finally burned completely through, as the wing abruptly separated and disintegrated. Within seconds, the hurtling, out of control machine plunged near vertically into rugged terrain in the Moors area of Central England. On impact, it shattered into tiny fragments, killing everyone aboard and sending a tremendous explosive shock wave rumbling across the English countryside.

On the flight back to Atlanta …

"Steve! Steve! Wake up! You're having one of those nightmares again!" Kay insisted, shaking him aggressively to assure that he was fully awakened. "You were quite fitful and getting a bit vocal."

"Oh … okay, thank you. Did I wake you up?" he asked.

"No. I've been awake the whole time, watching you. You really should try and go back to sleep after you calm down, if you can. You need it more than I do. Just try to think about something positive if at all possible." Kay suggested, as Steve nodded in agreement, leaned once more against the airliner's side window, and in less than a minute was fast asleep again.

June 13, 1945, 15:35 Hrs., Air Transport Command, U.S. Army Air Corps., Base Air Depot 2, Lancashire, England.

A thin smile began to form on Ed Hickey's taut face as he glanced at his watch and envisioned the sequence of events that must surely have happened by now. No doubt, the explosive charges had left their mark and the airplane and its crew were both just a memory, another unsolved mystery of the sea, never to be seen or heard from again. "So much for that little problem." he said, sporting a satisfied, wicked grin as he walked outside to the waiting truck. When he reached it, he climbed into the front seat for the long drive back to Stafford shire, England. He was anxious to forget the James Tyree Crew and return to his other O.S.S. duties.

June 25, 1945, 16:25 Hrs., Regional Headquarters, Office of Strategic Services, London, England.

"Okay, Nate, let's hear it again one more time from the top." Tom Sturnman coached. "How many actually knew about Hickey's plan from the beginning?"

"Uh, well, like I said, sir, it was a last minute thing. We were just going to delay them in the beginning." Nate Watson replied.

"We understand that, Nate, and we appreciate your coming in here and being so up front about all of it." Sturnman continued.

"But we've got a real problem on our hands. I'm sure you've heard by now that the airplane came down in the Moors area of central England."

"No, sir!" Watson gasped, staring at him in shocked disbelief.

"Well, now you know! Eighth Air Force recovery teams are crawling all over the wreckage right now as we speak." Sturnman declared. "And you know what else they're doing, Nate?"

"No, sir."

"Accident investigation! Accident investigation, Nate! And how long do you think it will take them to figure out that the airplane exploded in-flight? Not long, I can assure you!" he taunted.

"Sir, I …"

"Silence!" Sturnman snapped, cutting him off immediately.   "You see, Nate, we've got a hell of a mess on our hands, a hell of a mess, thanks to Hickey and the rest of you."

"Sir …"

"One we're going to have to clean up and somehow erase permanently!" Sturnman continued.

"How … how do we do that, sir?" Nate Watson asked meekly, still staring straight ahead, as Sturnman gradually walked around the room behind him.

"By tying up all the loose ends, Nate!" Sturnman replied, pulling out his Colt .45 automatic pistol and firing it into the back of Watson's head at point-blank range.

July 19, 1945, 16:44 Hrs., St. Agathe D'Aliermont, Pas-De-Calais Area, Northern Coast of France.

As they settled in for another day of waiting outside the O.S.S. safe house, Tom Sturnman and Phil Osterhouse scanned the street for any sign of movement. Ten days of staking out the safe house with no sign of Ed Hickey had made Sturnman doubt his own instincts. He knew Hickey was hiding somewhere and had not attempted to contact the organization since June 12th. He also knew there were few places a loner like Hickey could go. He certainly had no friends to turn to or any other support within the O.S.S. In fact, Ed Hickey was more alone and isolated than any man Sturnman had ever known.

After waiting endless hours inside the two door sedan, Sturnman's attention was suddenly drawn to a distant solitary figure at the bottom of the narrow street walking cautiously in their direction. The short, slightly built male was approaching discreetly, glancing nervously over his shoulder at regular intervals. "Hey, take a look!" Sturnman exclaimed, nudging Phil Osterhouse and nodding at the figure in the distance.

"Is that him?" Osterhouse asked curiously.

"Could be. He's got Hickey's build."

"He sure seems nervous about something."

"Wouldn't you be?" Sturnman asked, checking his .45 automatic. "Let's take him before he gets inside the safe house!" he ordered, opening the car door and stepping out into the street as Osterhouse followed. The moment they did, both men flinched instinctively as a high powered rifle erupted across the street and the concussion shook them forcefully. Recovering within moments, Sturnman saw a lone gunman hidden inside a doorway across the street firing intently at the man in the distance. Hit badly, the man fell to the street as the unrelenting gunman fired again. Without hesitating, Sturnman reacted to the attack, taking quick aim with his .45 automatic and emptying it into the gunman inside the doorway. The huge .45 slugs tore into the gunman mercilessly, snapping his head back and dropping him to the ground as Sturnman quickly reloaded the weapon. Eyeing the assassin's target, Sturnman saw he had fallen face down in the street and was now twitching badly as his body reacted to the shock of being hit.

Sweeping the area with his .45, Sturnman shouted at Phil Osterhouse. "Finish him!" gesturing at the wounded gunman in the doorway as he eased toward the other man. When he reached him, he kneeled down and rolled him over. His instincts had been right! Sturnman was suddenly face to face with Ed Hickey.

"Ed! Ed! It's me, Tom Sturnman!" he declared, grasping Hickey's head and elevating it slightly.

"Tom? Tom? What are you doing here?" Hickey gasped, coughing up blood and wincing in pain.

"Looking for you. Who was shooting at you, Ed?" he asked bluntly, as he watched Hickey gasp for air through a massive chest wound.

"How … how bad am I hurt?" Hickey cried out.

"Just take it easy, Ed. Help is on the way." Sturnman lied, flinching again as Osterhouse finished the lone gunman with a single pistol shot to the head. "Who was shooting at you, Ed?" he repeated.

Gasping, Hickey managed, "He was with the other man I shot here before. I've been followed for days."

"Is that why you stayed away from the safe house?" Sturnman asked pointedly, as Hickey managed to nod. "What were you thinking about with that bomber crew, Ed? What made you do that?" he demanded, searching Hickey's face for some kind of reaction, some sign of remorse. But there was none. Completely unemotional, Hickey just gasped, "the shipment. I was protecting the shipment."

"You killed twenty-seven innocent Americans and one of our own agents." Sturnman shot back accusingly, as his eyes bore into Hickey.

Ignoring the charge, Hickey sneered, "you and your damn Paris meeting! I did what you told me to do. How … how bad am I hurt? What about me? What about me, Tom?"

Removing his hand from under Hickey's neck and standing back up, Sturnman stared at him in silence for a moment before answering. "Oh, you're hurt pretty bad, Ed, but you'd probably make it if we got you to a good hospital right away. You'd probably make it, and we just can't have that, Ed."

"Tom?" Hickey exclaimed, recoiling as Sturnman leveled the .45 automatic at his head. "Tom?" he screamed, as Sturnman released the safety.

On the flight back to Atlanta …

"Steve! Steve! You need to wake up! You were fidgeting badly again and having another nightmare. You probably should stay awake for the rest of the flight. We're supposed to be landing in Atlanta in about twenty-five minutes." Kay stated.

"Huh? Oh … okay." he said sleepily, trying to clear his head from the physical and emotional trauma implanted in him by the transference process.

"Another really bad one, huh?" Kay asked tentatively.

"It was like I was actually there in 1945, experiencing everything that everyone at the time did mentally and physically. Every sensation I have is so unbelievably real!" he exclaimed.

"I think what might help lower the intensity of this kind of experience is to focus your mind on unconditional forgiveness, like Uncle Wohali suggested. It probably won't completely dull all your sensations, but it should definitely reduce the magnitude of the overall experience and the frequency of the visions." she stated.

"That makes sense, if I can just do it. The vividness and trauma of the visions makes any degree of forgiveness a major emotional challenge. If anybody can teach me a lesson about forgiveness though, it's Native-Americans like Uncle

Wohali. No question about it, Native-Americans have more to forgive other people for than most of us will ever know." he said emphatically.

"Well, the Bible says that we all have to learn to forgive others if we want to be forgiven for our own sins." Kay replied. "We must learn to show mercy and forgiveness if we want our Holy Father in Heaven to show us mercy and forgiveness."

"I know … I know. It's just such an uphill battle with everything implanted so deeply in my subconscious and ready to unleash every time I close my eyes. Sometimes, I even see it all happening in the background when I'm wide awake. I can't make those images go away by waking up or by simply demonstrating forgiveness." he reasoned.

"No, but you must ask your Heavenly Father for the strength to not overreact to the stimuli within the visions and for a heart that is willing to unconditionally forgive such an atrocity."

"That's just it … the experience is so real each time that I feel like it's actually happening to me. It's like reliving my own airplane crash and murder, over and over again." he said somberly.

"Well, I can tell you that none of that matters on the other side of the veil. Over there, you see things from an entirely different perspective and there is no fear of death or desire for revenge. The real James Tyree Bomber Crew isn't sitting around reliving this tragedy or plotting their revenge. Those are earthly emotions and they have no place in the heavenly realm. The dark side only uses them to cause more pain and suffering on Earth. If the Native-Americans are able to rise above all that and forgive the horrible suffering and injustice imposed on them by humanity, I believe everyone can find the inner strength to forgive a major transgression."

"That's pretty hard to argue against. The trials and tribulations of Native-Americans make my visions and sleepless nights look rather tame comparatively." he stated.

"You and I shared our insight with the Cherokee people about discerning evil spirits, especially those masquerading as angels of light. Now, you should let the Cherokee people teach you how to forgive others and remain pure of heart in a world that has taken everything you love away from you, including your hope for the future. Native-Americans are essentially the modern day equivalent of *Job*. The Biblical story of *Job* is an account of tremendous personal suffering, galactic loss, and yet enduring faith in the Great Spirit. Whether we follow the Biblical example of *Job,* or the modern day example of Native-Americans, we can all benefit spiritually from such wonderful examples of how to forgive. The ability to forgive is what enables us to put all the traumas of life behind us and move on as we surrender all our concerns to the Great Spirit.

Of course simply knowing how to forgive doesn't mean that Native-American people have lost their ability to still be mighty warriors here on Earth. The Navajo code talkers of World War II proved that by greatly contributing to the Allies success against the Japanese in the Pacific Islands campaign. It's understanding the spiritual balance between unconditional forgiveness and mastering earthly conflict when it becomes necessary that makes Native-American people so special."

"I know at least one that's pretty special." he replied, eyeing her affectionately. "I'm certain that acquiring such an advanced ability to forgive is going to be tremendously challenging for me. It's impossible for me to forget the injustice done to the James Tyree Bomber Crew, even when I'm sound asleep. I only wish that it wasn't so easy for the rest of the world to forget their sacrifice day and night; even going so far as to dismiss it outright."

"The Lord doesn't want the world to forget any meaningful sacrifice. His Son was the epitome of a meaningful sacrifice that everyone needs to honor and remember. Our Heavenly Father requires us to demonstrate forgiveness, not forgetfulness. I know the Cherokee people will never forget the *Trail of Tears* or what Jesus went through to earn their salvation. Now, because of what we just shared with the Cherokee people, they will never forget the sacrifice of the James Tyree Bomber Crew. All of us are united by pain, suffering and sacrifice as long as we're in this earthly realm. But, if we walk in the spirit, we will not submit to the dark side or the weakness of the flesh." Kay offered reassuringly.

"I hope you're right. After all this, it would be a downright shame for the darkness to prevail just because the world continued to turn a blind eye to the sacred gift they were offered by so many brave men." he said sadly, pausing after he spoke to scan outside the aircraft's side window. "I know in my heart that you're absolutely right of course. But … I have to wonder what my Uncle Ray would think if he saw his Service Bible on display at the Cherokee Heritage Center in Oklahoma?"

"From my experience beyond the veil, I would say that he would be pleased to see the eternal hand of God in all of it, just as we should be." she declared.

"Amen … I couldn't have said it better. We better get fastened in now. It looks like there are going to be a few bumps on the descent into Atlanta, but the good news is … this flight should be landing right on schedule!"

Choctaw Spiritual Prayer

Oh Great Spirit Father, Creator of all life below, please hear my spiritual prayer. For I seek guidance in a world where few can lay claim to eternal peace.

Grant me the vision to see beyond tomorrow's horizon, yet still accept my daily trials, that must and will be faced to survive.

Give me the strength to rise each day and breathe the breath of life that you have provided for me.

Touch my spiritual soul, so that I may use every moment to spread your sacred message of love and peace for all mankind.

I ask only the privilege to speak my native tongue, and learn the ways of my people, from generations of old.

Help me to understand and accept that we are of one body, as each spirit flows, from one to another in a sacred hoop.

Let the trails that bore my ancestors blood and tears, and the chains that bound their freedom serve as reminders to all, of our hate and savagery against one another, and ensure its trust that we as a people choose never to repeat such ignorance.

Grant Mother Earth the strength to endure all injustices that have been placed upon her, and cleanse her red clay body to renew her growth for new generations to thrive.

Embrace my mind and grant me the wisdom to seek and receive my ancestral birthright.

Guide my feet down the passage of forgiveness, of those who have severed my tribal ties, and help me to bind them once more.

Teach this child, oh Great One, the true lesson of life, its sacred message of love, to spread freely beyond self, and among my brothers and sisters throughout the duration of my earthly existence.

May your morning sun awaken this weary body, and your night moon allow it to meditate and rest. May your spirit continue to heal and instill within me the meaning of this spiritual prayer, and trust that I use it to serve you well.

www.ingramcontent.com/pod-product-compliance
Lightning Source LLC
Chambersburg PA
CBHW082050220626
47052CB00006B/1197